All the Time There Is

All the Time There Is

Toby Stein

Random House New York

Library of Congress Cataloging in Publication Data
Stein, Toby.
All the time there is.

I.   Title.
PZ4.S8197A1   [PS3569.T3754]   813'.5'4   76-53532
ISBN 0-394-41160-9

Manufactured in the United States of America

9 8 7 6 5 4 3 2

First Edition

For Lady Zam and Louis,
who left me love:
may they dwell in the house of the Lord forever

A Beginning:
November

HE FIXED DAIQUIRIS FOR US while I leaned against the open shutter-door and watched. The small kitchen, mirror layout of my own across the hall, was slightly too decorated for my taste. But if the kitchen looked like something in a magazine, the smells filling it at the moment were those of serious real-life cooking: garlic, and not too little of it, and broccoli and some on-the-tip-of-my-tongue cheese. Gorgonzola! Of course! I liked the smells, each of them, all of them together.

I liked the way he worked, too, as though I weren't there. He used his hands sparingly. They were rather wide, almost stubby hands, certainly not what you would call beautiful hands. But the way the left hand seemed to know exactly what the right hand was doing—that you might call beautiful. To me it was.

He rolled the plump lime between his palms, cut it in half, and worked the halves firmly against the ridged center of the old-fashioned glass juicer until there was only damp pulp left. He poured the juice into the blender. Then he measured four jiggers of the requisite Mount Gay rum into the blender, letting the fourth jigger overflow for good measure. He dipped a teaspoon into a large jar of honey, and after patiently letting it drip level, added it to the mixture in the blender and then repeated the measure, scrupulously transferring

3

every clinging bit of the thick rich sweetness from the spoon to the blender with the most efficient utensil, a finger. Finally, he measured in two teaspoons of sugar.

"Perfect, I should think," I said.

"A reliable source," he said, and pressed a button, and the liquid whirred and rose and frothed in the blender. It was as pleasant and hypnotic to watch as a campfire. As I stared into the whitened whirling liquid, I could already taste it, and I smiled because people said there was some good in everyone and I wondered if a recipe for superb daiquiris counted.

He got ice cubes out, and placing them in a clean dishtowel, he held the bulky mound steady against the sink edge with one hand while shattering the cubes with half a dozen well-aimed blows of a small metal hammer. Laying the filled towel on the counter, he removed from the freezer the champagne glasses he had dipped into confectioner's sugar when he placed them in there to chill before we'd set out for our walk. He emptied the shaved ice into the glasses, worked the blender again, letting it whirl for three or four seconds, and poured the foaming daiquiris over the ice. Then he turned and handed me the drinks.

"I'll be in in a minute," he said.

I nodded and went into the living room. I placed both glasses side by side on the coffee table and settled myself into the pliant leather of the sofa.

As usual he was punctual. Coming into the living room, he glanced at the stereo system and then at me.

"Only if it goes with frozen daiquiris in November," I said.

He nodded, bent to the records, and after a moment selected something. He placed three records on the turntable. As he walked toward me, the gaily frosted Bach began.

"No fair," I said. "The Brandenburgs go with anything."

He sat down beside me. "When you say a long walk, you mean a long walk," he said, putting his feet up on the table, well clear of the glasses.

"What's in the oven?"

"A surprise," he said.

"It smells marvelous—and ready."

"It is, but I've turned the oven down to two hundred and it'll keep practically forever." He reached over his legs and picked up both glasses. "Unless you want to eat right away?"

I shook my head. "Good," he said, handing me one of the drinks. Then he raised his glass toward me. "Happy birthday," he said.

"Yes," I said. "It is."

We drank to that.

And then, sipping the daiquiris, we each went our own way on the Bach.

Nearly ten years ago. I had been making my way through a bowl of soup with dragging slowness, doing more stirring than eating. It was February and I couldn't seem to get warm, although there was plenty of heat coming up. There was Bach playing then, too: not the Brandenburgs, but the cantata *"Jauchzet Gott in allen Landen,"* which, that evening, struck me as unaccountably sad. I decided to change the record and was just putting on a Mozart horn concerto to spur me through the rest of the soup when the phone rang.

The phone hadn't rung in three days, so I was grateful, even before I answered it, to whoever was on the other end, excepting only an inaccurate dialer.

He had dialed correctly. It *was* me he wanted—he being someone I'd dated occasionally in college, newly divorced and bent on reactivating an acquaintance he apparently remembered as a relationship. He'd begun by offering his condolences, but since he'd never met Hal, and Hal had been dead nearly a year anyway, I didn't know what to say to that. So I said yes, I was free for dinner the following Friday.

He seemed to see himself as a restaurant critic of Arnoldian high seriousness. Despite an icy downpour and a taxi strike, he had insisted we go to an out-of-the-way, brand-new "in" restaurant. Word-of-mouth had it that in a month it would be *impossible* to get a table unless one's picture appeared with some regularity in *Women's Wear Daily.*

It was a pleasant place, understandably half empty given the weather. I had ordered my usual Kïr. But he had smiled and told the waiter to bring us both frozen honey daiquiris. In February. In a storm. I had considered leaving right then, but my feet were wet right through my brand-new suede boots, and it *was* warm in the restaurant and bitter outside. I stayed.

When the daiquiris arrived, my annoyance dissipated slightly because it was undeniably a pleasant drink. But he had sent his back, and although I protested, mine too. And then yet again, both of them, the second time with precise instructions scratched in ball-point pen on a linen napkin. As he wrote out the recipe, he simultaneously said it, loudly and clearly, as if to coerce me into being his witness, lest the third set of daiquiris arrive imperfect.

By the time they came, perfect, I was too angry to enjoy mine—but not so angry that I failed to realize I would, on another occasion, enjoy it thoroughly. A little later, when I sought refuge in the ladies' room during his onslaught on the Béarnaise, I jotted down the recipe on the inside cover of a book of matches. I stayed in the bathroom as long as I could before returning to the table, and then I stuck it out through a lengthy diatribe on the lighting and the service. But when he sent back the perfectly good espresso that I really wanted to drink, I got up, told him not to get up, and I walked out of there and hiked home. I had had to throw out my new boots the next day. The suede had turned to scrap iron overnight.

"You know," I said, turning to him, "suede boots never outlive a season anyway, but a good daiquiri recipe lasts forever."

"I was beginning to wonder where you'd gone," he said. "I'm glad it was only with him."

"You remember!" I was pleased. He had laughed when I told him the story on that summer evening when I introduced him to the daiquiris, and that had made me add details to it, some of them quite impromptu. Still, it had been months ago.

"Remember him? The worst disaster since the Bay of Pigs!" He raised an eyebrow into a bushy question mark. "The way you tell it, anyway. He wasn't really that bad, was he? I mean, not really?"

"*Really?*" I gave the question war-or-peace considera-
tion for a full twenty seconds.

"Really, he was half again as bad. He wore short
socks and had indecently hairy ears—and he wheezed."

"Last time he stuttered."

"He's gotten over that," I said, trying not to laugh.
And then, suddenly, I didn't feel at all like laughing.
"I know it sounds funny, but I don't remember *him*.
I remember the evening's embarrassments vividly, but
not his face or the way he dressed or . . . him."

He said, not looking at me but not seeming to look
away deliberately either, "I don't think that sounds
funny."

I was grateful to him for saying that, and then not,
because I couldn't think of anything to say in reply.
And I had to say something. So I said, "Frozen daiquiris
in November are not all that much saner than frozen
daiquiris in February, you know." My voice sounded
as if it needed tuning.

He didn't remark on that. He didn't say anything.
Instead, he put his arm around my shoulders and pulled
me a little closer to him. Then he kissed me. First,
on the side of my forehead, a kiss you could call comforting. It was a nice thing to do. Comforting, in fact.

Then, after a moment, he bent his head and kissed
the outside corners of my eyes, where I have lately
noticed a growing colony of what the world laughingly
calls laugh wrinkles. That wasn't quite as comforting.
I mean, I don't really mind them, but I don't exactly
crave attention being paid to them. Then he kissed
my eyes and, when I opened them again, my cheeks,
turning my head with his hand. And then he kissed
my lips. Brief, weightless kisses.

"Your lips taste sweet," he said, moving away just enough to look at me.

"The daiquiris," I said. I smiled, but my lips seemed to have only partial mobility.

"Of course," he said, and kissed me again, a longer kiss, but without pressure. He was saying something; he wasn't asking anything.

Then his lips moved down and lightly, ever so lightly, he kissed the hollow of my throat. And then he drew away again. Again, not far.

His thick grey-black eyebrows, strong punctuation in an otherwise mild face, were wedged close together. In his eyes the grey darkened to charcoal. It seemed that our bodies were in a holding pattern like that for a long time, while our eyes probed as far as they could inside each other.

He stood and reached out his hand for me and then we were standing very close, and his hands were in my hair and his mouth felt insistent on mine.

And I was kissing him, too. Our unopened lips met and pressed, again and again, as if looking for a secret door. It happened then: quite as if by magic, our mouths opened at exactly the same moment and our tongues entwined.

Instantly, it triggered a movement deep inside me. Prepared for everything but desire, I pulled away. I wanted to press my palms against my belly hard enough to stop the sweet spasms in there. But I just locked my hands together.

"Don't you want to?" he asked. I followed his eyes to my hands: the knuckles were drained of blood. The way he asked it, I sensed that if I said no, we could probably go on the way we had been. If I said yes, there was a good chance that there was no chance. If I said no, I didn't think he'd ask again. The only thing I knew for sure was that he was asking—now. I made myself look at him, at his darkened eyes and into them. Then I checked my gut, and because it was the truth, I *wanted* to, I nodded.

"All right, then," he said, and taking me firmly by the hand, led me into the bedroom.

I had been in that apartment a dozen times, but never in the bedroom. It was all in browns, even the walls were brown, plainly a male domain, and I felt strange in there. Immediately, I retrieved my hand and lost my composure. I sat down quickly on the bed, because I did not at once see the chair in the far corner and because I was unsure my legs would continue to remember how to stand. And if they were not up to doing that simple everyday act now, what hope was there for the rest of my body later?

He was standing in front of me, and there was really nothing I could do except look up at him. He looked . . . familiar. But we were *friends*. I began to shake.

He spoke very softly. "I could refill our glasses," he said. "There was some left."

Dumbly, I nodded, and he turned to go. He was going. "No, stay here!" I said, and it came out too loud. "Stay here," I said again, in what sounded to me like someone else's taut voice.

He stayed.

He sat down close beside me on the bed, but he didn't touch me or even look at me, not for quite a while. Eventually, my shaking slackened, and I was able to remember him. I looked at him.

"Are you okay?" he asked. I nodded. "We could eat

now, if you'd rather," he said. Then, hearing himself, I suppose, he smiled. I smiled and shook my head. He took my face in his hands and held it and looked at me and I felt at home. He kissed me gently, and then less gently, on my mouth and then on my neck. I stopped feeling at home, and began feeling. He was kissing my ear—it made me stir inside, and I bit my lip so as not to make a noise. I was trembling again, but if he had asked me if I was trembling more from fear than from feeling, I would not have been able to say. But he wasn't asking. His hand was on the zipper at the back of my dress, and he was unzipping it partway and slipping the dress off my shoulders.

"Oh!" he said. It was more an intake of breath than a word. With the tips of his fingers, delicately, as if I were made of marble and he knew how fragile marble really is, he traced the outline of my shoulders. I have always thought my shoulders were the best part of my body, and that helped me to sit straight and still and, finally, to stretch out my arms to him.

He took both my hands in one of his and with his other hand brought my chin close and kissed me again, opening my lips with his. His tongue, inside my mouth, felt large; it seemed to fill my whole mouth, and then I was wet.

Startled, I drew away. I needed a moment; I felt out of breath. He let me go. As I moved to the far side of the bed, I felt his eyes on me.

"I'll be back in a moment," he said, a roughness in his voice. He cleared his throat. "The casserole," he said, "I'd better make sure I did lower the oven," and went quickly out of the room.

I didn't know whether to laugh or cry. He didn't care

if the casserole dried out; I knew him well enough to know that. He was leaving to give me a chance to get undressed in private; he had taken my moving to where I now stood as assent.

Wasn't it?

Well, was it?

Moving as efficiently as my shaking fingers allowed, I took off my dress and slip and pantyhose. I had unhooked my bra and was slipping it off when he came back into the room. He turned to go out again.

"It's all right," I said. I dropped my bra on the floor, slipped off my panties, pulled back the heavy brown Spanish spread and blankets, and slipped between the sheets.

He came around to my side of the bed and sat down on the edge. "It's going to be all right," he said. He put his hand on the cover. "I want to look at you." I nodded.

He pulled back the covers and looked at me, at my body—deliberately, concentrating, taking his time. He started at my shoulders and worked his way down to my toes, touching me only with his eyes.

Then he bent his head to my lower belly and kissed his way into and through my pubic hair until his mouth found my clitoris, and his tongue, pointed and hot, flicked it and seared it and raised it until I quivered and arched my back and cried out for him.

Immediately, he nodded and stood, and without taking his eyes off mine, disposed of his clothes without a wasted motion. He came toward me, and as I moved toward the center of the bed to make room for him, in my excitement and tension I looked the one place I had determined not to look.

But it was all right: he was fully erect. Only then did I know how much of my trembling had been bound up with fear that he would not be ready when the time came. Joyously, I moved into his embrace and felt his body, hard and strong and urgent, pressed against the length of mine. Suddenly, in less time than can be told, the hardness was gone.

And the lifeblood went out of me, too.

The Beginning:
The April Before

1

THE CLICK OF THE AUTOMATIC LOCK on the door punctuated Mr. Shapley's exit.

"When are you going to sell him those candlesticks?" Munch asked without looking up from her paperwork.

"He's getting there." I replaced the Georgian candlesticks in their display case, relocked it, and pocketed the key.

"But two months!" Munch raised both her head and her eyebrows.

"O compassionate one," I said. "Mr. Shapley is going to get, those sticks for fifty dollars less than the first price I named. He knows that. Haggling over the price is his way of having us look at them together. Once he gets them home, the pleasure will be his alone. And, therefore, in Mr. Shapley's case, less."

"What if someone walks in and wants them at the ticketed price?" persisted Munch, named thus for no apparent reason, as she is even slimmer than I am and always has been, dating back at least to our freshman English class at Barnard.

I turned slightly away for a moment and then back to Munch, my face prepared. Mimicking my most professionally persuasive voice, I said, "I am sorry, but these candlesticks have just been purchased over the telephone." I lowered my voice to a stage whisper. "By the president of Costa Rica—through an intermediary of course." I lowered my voice yet another notch, to make Munch have to strain to hear me. "However, there is another pair I've just had the good fortune to acquire that no one—but no one—has even seen yet. I think you may agree they're a millimeter more splendid."

"You really wouldn't sell them to anyone else, would you?" Munch had grown exceedingly fond of Mr. Shapley; he had been our very first customer and she regarded him as an ambulatory good-luck charm.

"Now, how could I?"

The telephone beside Munch rang. "An intermediary of Uruguay's president?" She picked up the phone. "Hello," she said, stretching out the syllables like taffy pull.

"Hi Munch. Is Mom there?" Alex's loud voice invariably carried past her immediate audience.

"There's a lady here who fits that rough description." Munch held the receiver out to me. "It's your daughter, softie."

I took the phone. "Hello, darling."

"Mom, look, don't get mad. But please be on time and please don't wear pants. Okay?"

"Yes, ma'am."

"And don't be mad."

"No, ma'am."

"Mother!"

"Alex, I will be on time. I will not wear pants. I am not and will not be angry. But really—"

"Terrific! 'Bye." Alex was always on the run.

I looked at the dead receiver in my hand and slowly replaced it in its cradle. I sat down on the edge of Munch's desk. "Which is worse? Your daughter is trying to live off you, mine is trying to love through me. At least I think that's what's going on. Tonight I meet another prospect."

Munch took off her stylish metal-rimmed eyeglasses and rubbed the bridge of her nose. "I'd been getting the idea lately that Alex isn't as big on marriage as she used to be."

"*Her* marriage. My marriage she's still big on. Bigger. This one tonight's the second 'eligible' she's invited me to meet this month."

"You didn't say she told you she asked a man."

"She *told* me not to wear pants. And she told me she's making Chicken Kiev. For her mother alone, my daughter doesn't make Chicken Kiev."

"Maybe he'll be marvelous."

"Attractive as George C. Scott and as urbane as Peter Ustinov." I shook my head: unlikely. "Look," I added, "I haven't got any commitments on Wednesdays and if it makes Alex happy to try to—"

"Your exercise class is on Wednesday."

"I forgot to tell you?" I hadn't forgotten; I was just waiting until my pride had subsided. "I got promoted to advanced two weeks ago. Tuesdays and Thursdays."

"You're something."

"Sure. A middle-aged exercise prodigy."

"I mean it."

"I love you, too," I said. And bending over the desk, I added in my stand-by stage whisper, "I'll prove it. I'll tell you a secret. Alex makes Chicken Kiev with margarine."

I began to laugh. Munch began to laugh. We laugh a lot together. It helps.

2

HALF AN HOUR BEFORE CLOSING, two Arabs in pin-striped suits and Countess Mara ties had come in. They were looking for a present for their sister, who was getting married. They looked closely at half our stock; I could look forward to a morning of fingerprint removal. Eventually, they selected a white elephant—a complete rococo tea and coffee service I had grown to hate more every time I had to polish its eleven pieces.

Then they said they were interested in silverware. I showed them every set of antique silver in the shop, including at least two I wouldn't mind having myself, but they smilingly shook their heads over each one. Shyly, they said they had something *brighter* in mind. It turned out they had seen, in an uncle's villa back home, just the pattern they wanted. They even knew the name.

After trying to explain for fifteen minutes that we did not deal in new silverware, I was afraid they might change their minds about the silver white elephant they'd already chosen, so I took their order for service for seventy-two of Gorham's Versailles pattern in vermeil. It would be hard to come by that much of an out-of-date pattern, but I wasn't going to worry about it just then. I told them I'd have it in two weeks and wrapped their white elephant, for which they paid cash in new fifties. I coaxed them out the door, and put the money in the safe. By then I was running an hour and a half late.

I found a taxi immediately and had the fare and tip ready when it pulled up in front of my brownstone.

As I hurried up the outside steps, I struggled with my keys. Then I pushed open the outer door, got my mail, opened the inside door, and rushed up the stairs. Nearing the second-floor landing, I saw Charles Robinson, who lived in the other apartment on the floor, locking his door.

"Evening," I said, taking the top step and turning, in a single movement, toward my front apartment.

"Good eve—" Charles Robinson began as I rushed headlong into his roommate, Raymond Elliott, who deftly put out his hands and caught me.

"Sorry," he said, his reflexes as gracious as they were quick.

"*I'm* sorry. I wasn't looking . . . terrible hurry . . . going out to dinner . . . late . . ." I inhaled, looked up into Raymond Elliott's dark, delicately handsome face, and laughed.

He laughed with me. A nice laugh too, I noticed, having only noted previously that he had an appealing smile. Inclining his head a trifle ceremoniously, but smiling to place quotation marks around the movement, he ushered me in the direction of my apartment. "Have a good time!" he called as he followed Charles Robinson downstairs.

Opening my door, I called after them, "Thanks! You too." I went inside, kicking the door shut behind me and dropping my purse and mail on the table beside the door, and took a deep breath.

It was always the same, that moment after I entered my apartment.

There are times when I feel lonely here, or frustrated, or too tired to be either, but the first moment inside never fails me. My place. In a way, it's the first place

I've ever had that's all my own. I went from my parents' apartment to a college dorm; then, married the week after commencement, to an apartment. We moved to a larger apartment, then to a small house, and then to the house with the big kitchen for me and the honest-to-God den for Hal.

Each place had good memories, but this place is special because it is mine alone—the way I want it to look, the way I want it to feel.

Yes. The living room is neither exceptionally large nor small. Comfortable furniture. Not too much of it, either. I like space to move in—to look at. Best of all, I like my plants.

Visually, as they do for me emotionally, the plants prevail. A schefflera nudging the ceiling stands in a huge ceramic planter; fifteen small cacti line the rungs of a clear lucite ladder. Seven plants, including my sensationally lush aeschynanthus, hang from window brackets in lieu of draperies. Hal had always liked draperies; he said they made a room cozy at night, drawn against the outside world. I like to look out. There are Venetian blinds, which I had installed right up against the window, so that when they are drawn, my plants hang inside. All in all, there are sixty-four plants, a number of them propagated by me from cuttings cadged from friends.

The green of growing things may be the dominant color, but there is also some clear, warm red, some unfaded lavender and a touch of Chinese yellow. Bookshelves line one wall, filled in what appears to be haphazard fashion, but I can lay my hands instantly on any book I want. There's a certain overflow that doesn't fit into the bookcases, even on their sides, and these books lie on tables, mostly, and a few are stacked near a reading chair. There is, too, the week's pileup of the *Times*—sometimes two weeks'. It's not the tidiest room; I am not the tidiest person. But it's always clean because I like to be around clean things. So that's how things are here.

It's my place.

Barry, a terribly attractive journalist I knew briefly but intimately a couple of years ago, once said my place was just illegible enough to prohibit successful forgery. I thought that was rather poetic for an investigative reporter and told him so, whereupon he admitted to having been a closet poet since college. We stopped seeing each other shortly after that; but last Christmas, when I happened on a slim volume by my favorite obscure poet, an Australian named John Manifold, I sent it to him.

Anyway, my feeling about my apartment has as little to do with rhyme as reason. What I feel, when I come in the door, is the "thereness" of the place. In much the same way as, whenever I fly home from a vacation trip, I appreciate the astonishing panorama of New York at night, but what I really see is—home.

Enough. My two-minute submersion in the feeling had refreshed me as thoroughly as a twenty-minute nap in a darkened room might. I had to hurry now. I slipped out of the jacket of my pants suit and unbuttoned the trousers as I headed for the bedroom.

Twenty minutes later, dressed in a black mat jersey dress, a chiffon stole around my shoulders, I emerged from the house—into a medium-hard, gusting downpour.

Spotting an oncoming cab with its roof lighted to indicate availability, I started down the stairs to hail it, but the steps were slippery and I had high-heeled sandals on, and the cab drove on past before I could catch it. As I stood at the curb, two occupied cabs went by and then a rush of raining wind blew my chiffon stole across my face. I was pulling at the clinging, blinding chiffon when a voice said, "Lady?"

I disentangled myself to find a cab in front of me. I got inside quickly, and sighed. "Hello!" I said. "Am I glad to see you—I mean, am I glad you saw me."

The cabbie, young and full-bearded, raised two fingers in the peace salute and smiled at me. He had about eighty very white teeth. "Now that we've met," he said, "where are we going?"

When the cab swashed to a stop in front of Alex's building, the meter read $4.15. I put a ten in the money slot and started to get out.

"Hey, wait," said the cabbie, "that was a ten."

I bent my head back inside the cab and peered through the bullet-proof shield at his identification card. "Arthur Gottlieb," I said, "Happy Chanukah."

"It's April," he said, just as a point of fact.

"Just in case I don't see you before December," I said.

As I watched my son-in-law Tom pouring after-dinner brandies across the room, I could feel Ed Flight watching me. Obviously uncomfortable in a low-slung artificial-leather chair, whose undulating outline conflicted with his considerable bulk, he had been watching me since we'd come back into the living room. During dinner he had concentrated on the food. I felt like the next course.

As Tom started toward us with the tray of brandies, I shot a glance at Ed. I had momentarily considered the possibility that his stare had been removed, like a hair in the eye, and what I was feeling was only the aftereffects of the intrusion. But no, he was still right in there. I picked up my cigarette case, took out a cigarette, and looked for the lighter that was usually on the table by my side.

"I hope you're not expecting me to light that for you."

"I can manage, thank you," I said, and got my own lighter out of my bag.

"You want to know why?"

I lighted my cigarette, wondering why his voice, which was rather deep and mellifluous, grated on me. I had no interest in why this stranger was making an issue about not lighting my cigarette, but Alex had made such a big effort that I made a small one and said, pleasantly enough, "You take women's liberationists at their word?"

"Laugh, go on," he said, and I knew why his voice annoyed me. The tone he took was inordinately intimate.

"I wasn't laughing." I listened, as carefully as if I had just made a recording, to my own voice. It was commendably matter-of-fact.

"You were joking. Same thing."

"You could say that, I suppose," I said, just to end it.

"What I could say—" Ed began, and was interrupted by Tom walking between us with the tray of brandies.

I took a glass from the tray and smiled up at my son-in-law, whom I liked at all times but whom I suddenly felt sensationally fond of because he was the least little bit bland. "Thank you, Tom," I said to him; and then, to Ed, not warmly, "By all means, do tell us."

Tom turned and offered the tray to Ed, who took a glass and said loudly, "Why don't you just stop!" Tom took a hasty step backward and spilled some of the two remaining brandies.

I waited until Tom had recovered his balance, set the tray down and taken his own drink before I looked squarely at Ed and said, very quietly, "Excuse me?"

"Smoking!"

I glanced at my cigarette, took a deliberately deep puff, and spoke through the smoke I blew in Ed's direction. "Oh, yes," I said.

"That all you have to say?"

I took a sip of brandy, puffed on my cigarette, and put it out as I considered the alternatives. Then I nodded.

"It'll kill you!" He flushed with anger.

I had had enough of this conversation and turned to Tom, who sat perched on the edge of the sofa, looking as if he were an uninvited guest in his own home. "Where's Alex?" The least my daughter the marriage broker could do was witness the conflagration caused by her match.

Tom jumped up, only too glad to escape. "I'll check."

"Never mind. Stay!" I ordered, not wanting to be left alone with Ed. "She'll be here in a minute, I'm sure," I said, trying to alleviate my son-in-law's obvious disappointment. "She gets detoured."

"You're just like her!" announced Ed.

"Like daughter, like mother."

As if on cue, Alex entered, carrying a tray with coffee. Ed pointed a dismissing finger at her. "Note *her!* Helen!"

Alex, hampered by the gracelessness of the militantly

thin, nearly dropped the tray she carried. Tom jumped up again, eager to get away from the immediate scene of battle. He made her give him the tray, which he then thumped down on the coffee table, spilling the cream.

"Tom!"

"I was only trying to help."

"I would have managed."

I managed a tight smile as I turned my attention to Ed, in an attempt to call everyone's attention away from the domestic scene. "Excuse me," I said, "I think I missed your train of thought."

"I told her! Every intelligent woman gets a Pap smear regular, I said. I told her! By the time she went, you know what they found?"

I stifled a flippancy before it reached my lips. The man was upset. "Your wife died of cancer? I am sorry."

"You should be sorry! You're just like her. Two of a kind."

"Mr. Flight, not that it's any of your business, but I do happen to get a Pap smear—regular."

"Go on, mock me! You'll see! You want to die? You want to suffer?"

I glanced at Alex, who was pouring coffee as if my conversation with Ed Flight were in Russian. The vagrant last straw landed. Alex handed me my coffee. I placed the cup on the coffee table, and stood.

I looked directly at Ed. "No, not any more, thank you."

"Mother!" said Alex in a peculiarly high voice.

" 'Mother' is why I came," I said. "But it's not a good enough reason to prolong this visit," I told my daughter. "Tom, may I have my stole?"

"Mother, just stay a little while . . ." Alex had no flair whatever for coping with a scene not of her own making. But in fact, this scene *was* hers. And I was going to leave her to it.

At the door of the living room, Tom waited with my stole, which he placed around my shoulders.

"It's dry," he said, to say something I guess.

"It's been a long evening," I said to him, not, I hope, unkindly.

Ed, who had managed to disengage himself from the Naugahyde recesses of his chair, was starting toward me. I took a step backward. Luckily for Tom, he had stepped aside to open the door for me.

"Wait, Anne. I'm seeing you home!" said Ed, advancing on me.

"Mr. Flight, you'll see me dead first," I said. And then Tom took me down and put me in a cab. Which unfortunately was driven by someone other than Arthur Gottlieb.

3

THERE ARE TWO KINDS OF PEOPLE IN THE WORLD, it seems to me. People who talk to their plants, and people who think people who talk to their plants are a little leafy.

I am a card-carrying Type #1. Whereas my close

friends might admit that I am subject to certain vagaries, I doubt that any of them would grant that I am mad beyond your run-of-the-social-rat-race, on her own, pushing-middle-age-but-not-strenuously widow lady.

Talking to plants isn't crazy talk. It makes good sense, if you happen to grasp the nature of answers. Talk to a plant, it will not answer you. But it will grow in a window that faces the wrong light; or it will grow half again as fast as the plant-store man promised; or it will temporarily survive pestilence and/or plague even if you happen to be out of town on the weekend it comes down with same. It responds.

An Episcopalian convert friend of mine once put it this way: talking to a plant is rather like talking to God. He also does not respond to a conversational gambit in kind, but he responds. Does God grow? I asked. One of you grows, she said.

One of you grows. I like that.

In the case of my plants, I'm not sure but that we haven't all grown some.

Of course, talk alone doesn't account for my plants' exuberant good health. Each morning I water the ones which want watering and am careful not to water the ones which don't. Before I leave for work I turn the radio on to a station which plays classical music all day.

Having completed the foregoing ritual on the morning after Ed Flight à la Kiev, I was locking my door, purse and garbage bag in delicate balance, when Raymond Elliott left his apartment, also carrying a bag of garbage.

"Sixish!" he called over his shoulder as the door closed after him. Seeing me, he said, "Good morning," and ushered me down the stairs ahead of him.

At the bottom, Raymond squirmed unobtrusively ahead of me and got the door. The outer door as well. When we reached the garbage cans, he raised the cover of one with exaggerated gallantry and I, enjoying his playfulness, demurely deposited my bag of garbage inside. He placed *his* bag of garbage on top of mine and closed the lid with a flourish. We both laughed.

"Thank you, kind sir."

"*De rien, madame,*" said Raymond Elliott in a voice that contained a bow from the waist, and added in his normal voice, "Have a nice dinner last night?"

"Don't ask and I won't tell you!"

"I don't *have* to ask, then. I've been there," he said.

"It seems funny now, but—"

"You're never going again."

I laughed. "Not this week anyway."

"I know just what you mean," he said, raising a hand in salute, and we turned in opposite directions.

I was polishing the samovar as Munch and I talked. I happened to glance over at her; surprise tinted her face.

"If I'd stayed, I'd have become ruder."

"Have you called Alex?" Munch asked.

"Not yet. You know, another half-hour of that man and I'd *have* died. God!"

Munch bit the end of her pencil. "Alex is so inept at matchmaking, you'd think she'd give it up."

"No chance. She won't rest until she's married off her poor widowed mother to somebody."

"Then why doesn't she come up with *somebody*?"

I rubbed away at the samovar for a moment. "Oh, they haven't all been so awful. It could be me, you know."

"No, it couldn't!" Munch, always loyal and true, was sure.

"Maybe I want too much," I, who wasn't sure, said. "Like chains of emeralds."

I smiled; Munch didn't look as though I'd smiled. I laid down the chamois. Munch was my oldest, dearest friend. "Like somebody pleasant, intelligent, independent —and *there* in a pinch!

Munch, who was not only my best friend but who teared easily, blinked. "Even throwing in a modest emerald or two, it doesn't sound so far-fetched to me."

"Evidently it must be." I picked up the chamois and worked at the spigot of the samovar, to give Munch a moment. When I looked over at her again, she was okay.

I said, aiming for medium levity, "It's not so bad living alone. After nearly eleven years you get used to it. I mean, it's got its advantages. You can eat chicken legs four nights in a row, nobody minds. You can leave your clean pantyhose over the shower rail until you wear them again. You can stay in bed all day Sunday if you feel like it. All you need is the *Times* delivered."

Seeing the expression on Munch's face, I shut up. I looked at the cloth in my hand, but it had nothing to offer. After a moment, I shrugged. "So it's not so terrific," I said. I began to buff the samovar, hard.

Most friends would have said something comforting. Something. But Munch is a better friend than that.

4

"MY NAME IS PHILIP ANDERWAY," he said.

"Anne Durham," I said.

It felt foolish, sitting there, telling each other our names.

It's something I frequently do, go to a concert alone, especially on Sunday afternoons. I don't mind going alone; like museums and unlike plays, I enjoy it more as a solitary activity. I don't like to feel that I have to dilute my concentration in order to be sociable between movements or even the halves of a concert.

Although we never exchanged glances, I had felt as early as the middle of the first movement of the "Jupiter" that the man seated to my right was listening to the same music I was. It's a rare experience. About as unusual and exciting as unexpectedly coming across someone who believes in the same God you do.

During the intermission I went out quickly, past the couple seated to my left. I felt disoriented. When a hand held a light to my cigarette, I knew before I looked up that it was he.

He was grey-haired and grey-eyed, a distinguished-looking man in his mid-fifties. Handsome, really. He was not smiling.

"Thank you," I said.

He nodded, but said nothing. I could think of nothing to say that wouldn't sound perfectly ridiculous, so I smoked in silence. He didn't move away, and when the bell rang we walked back into the hall more or less together.

Walking out, after the erratic second half of the program, we ended up beside each other again, at least partly by chance. "The Vivaldi was a little heavy-handed, don't you think?"

He looked at me. "Yes, exactly," he said.

We reached the head of the aisle. He was obviously not going to say anything more, and I had said quite enough. I turned to move toward an exit to my right.

But I could not go anywhere. The crowd was stationary. I felt a hand touch my elbow. It could have been a mistake, but I turned. He was standing very close to me.

"Would you join me for a cup of coffee?" he asked somberly.

I looked at his face, so serious above mine, and then swiveled my head around at the pressing crowd. "If you can get us out of here," I said.

"Do you often come alone to concerts here?" he asked.

"Quite often."

"I've never seen you," he said. His voice was factual, not flirtatious. "Are you a professional musician?"

"No," I said, "but what a nice thing to say."

The waitress came for our order. He had coffee and I asked for Darjeeling tea and he ordered an assortment of pastries. Then he looked across the table at me for a concentrated moment before he said, "It was the way you listened. Sometimes I wonder why some people go to concerts."

I hid my delighted amazement—a feat it's taken me forty-three years to achieve to a modest degree. "They're only half there," I said. "Are you?"

"Half there? Oh, I see, a musician. No. I play the piano after a fashion, but I'm far from being a musician. I'm a lawyer."

"What kind?"

"A good one," he said without smiling.

"I know," I said without thinking.

"How do you know?" He still wasn't smiling.

Instinct? The straightness of your eyes? The way you pay attention to music? "When I was a kid," I said, "I once won one of those contests where you have to guess how many sour balls are in a big jar."

"How many were there?"

"Eight hundred ninety-two."

"Did you get it on the button?"

"Yes!"

"What was the prize?"

"I don't remember."

He laughed. "But you remember the number of sour balls."

I thought about that for a moment. "That was the special part—guessing, I mean. I suppose the prize wasn't very special. What sort of law do you practice?"

"I have a feeling if I say corporate law, you'll be disappointed."

Yes. "Why should I be disappointed?"

"No need to be. I'm involved in two kinds of law— estate, which pays the bills, and a certain small practice

I'd call constitutional for want of a more modest word."

"I'm glad," I said.

"You're amazing," he said. "What do you do?"

"For a living? A friend of mine and I have a small antique-silver shop."

"Is that interesting?"

"I enjoy it. I love fine silver, and I rather like the selling part. Munch, that's my friend, does all the hard work—the books, accounts, that kind of thing."

The waitress brought our order and twice more we had seconds on coffee and tea. The next time the waitress approached our table, Philip Anderway raised his eyebrows questioningly at me. "I couldn't possibly," I said.

"I'm afraid I can't, either," he said. "The check, please," he said to the waitress. While she added it up, he glanced at his watch. "I'm afraid I've kept you unconscionably long as it is," he said.

"Not at all." I wanted to be more articulate than that. I wanted to say that not only was there no place I had to be right then, but also there was no place I'd rather be. Instead, I just said, "Really, no."

Philip Anderway left a few bills on the table and we walked out into the early evening breeze.

He turned to me. "A taxi?" he asked, and I was almost certain I heard reluctance in his voice, but how could I be sure I wasn't imagining it or succumbing to wishful thinking? Besides, he knew my name. He would ask if my phone were listed, I knew he would. I nodded. "Please," I said.

He raised his hand and instantaneously a taxi pulled to a screeching halt in front of us. When you need them, they're never around; when you'd just as soon have five more minutes to batten down the future, they appear with the immediacy of a bad itch. Philip Anderway was holding the door for me. I got in. There was still time for him to say something. He bent his head to the window of the taxi. I rolled down the window.

"I'd like very much to see you again," he said, and I was smiling as he added, "But I can't. Goodbye."

He quickly pulled his head back from the taxi window and moved away from the curb. Numbly, slowly, I started to roll up the window.

"Okay, lady, where to?"

5

I WANTED TO TELL MUNCH about Philip Anderway. But what was there to tell? A man who happened to have the seat next to me at a concert Sunday afternoon invited me for a cup of coffee afterward and we talked through three cups of tea, and then he put me in a taxi?

I could have told her that when I arrived home, I scoured the stove, washed my hair, did my nails, and when the phone rang late in the evening, spilled a cup of tea in my hurry to answer it.

"Hello!" I said, and my voice sounded as unfamiliar as the voice on the other end of the phone, "What? No, this is three-four-*five*-two . . . That's all right," I lied.

I could have told Munch that then, finally, I cried. Wept. As though someone had died.

It wasn't that I couldn't tell Munch all of that. I can tell Munch anything. It's just that, with some *uncomical* incidents, too, you really have to be there.

So I didn't tell Munch, or anyone.

It really does help, I've found, when the ordinary cataclysms of life strike, to have things to do. Not busywork suggested by well-meaning friends, but tried-and-true things you really like doing. Then, during a time when you don't *want* to do anything, you can do them by rote, without expression, so to speak. They make the minute hand catch up with the hour hand.

My exercise class is like that. It's a big thing in my life, that exercise class. I'm good. Maizie, our teacher, is one tough taskmaster, but she's as quick to praise as to berate. She says we're each our own competitors, and it's because of that that I'm proud of how I'm doing.

There was a time when I wasn't any competition at all—for myself or for anyone else—not when it came to anything requiring physical coordination. As an adolescent I had been as awkward as a wallflower gladiolus stuck alone in a vase. When a boy would ask me to dance occasionally (and most boys had antennae that directed them to other potential partners), I would say I don't dance. Not one of them ever said, not one, what do you mean? come! dance with me and you'll be dancing. Instead, they took me at my word, and passed out of my evening and my life.

At Barnard, dances were not obligatory but athletics

was. I took beginning tennis four times, beginning archery twice, and then switched to an innovative course called Relaxation. There was, the instructor would explain in the hushed atmosphere of the Relaxation Room, no skipping. First you had to relax the right wrist. I never could. I passed tennis and archery and Relaxation; attendance was mandatory but achievement was not. And I *went*. I never cut a class in four years. But I swore, the way a seven-year-old may swear that he will never never never drink milk when he grows up, that I would never even be in the same vicinity as a sport again once I graduated.

Some grownups never do drink milk; I maintained my athletics abstinence for a long time. Hal was the first man I ever danced with; it was our first New Year's Eve together and I had had three drinks. Hal had had a couple more. I had just enough sense remaining to realize it wouldn't matter how badly I danced. It didn't: not to me and, apparently, not to him.

From time to time I wondered whether my ungainliness would carry over into bed. Frankly, four months before our marriage, when I went to bed with Hal for the first time, which was also my first time with anyone, I soon became quite intoxicated by the way he moved me . . . to move. I think in baseball it's called being a natural.

I saw no reason to suppose that because my body did not fail me in bed, it might have possibilities on some other playing field. Some months after Hal's death, when a number of fulsome sexual encounters forced me to look at my body other than in a mirror, in desperation I signed up for a beginner's swimming class in a "Y" clear across town. There, where there was no chance I would encounter anyone I knew, I dared for the first time in my life to try to get my body on my side.

After the first lesson, I cried when I got home. After the second lesson, I cried when I got home. But I kept going back: I *required* it of me.

Two months later I swam well enough to register at my neighborhood "Y" for an intermediate class.

In the ten and a half years since then, I have become a strong swimmer, learned to play a middling game of tennis, tried Yoga with some success, and even studied T'ai Chi Chuan for six months recently. The plain exercise class turned out to be what suits me best: there's no philosophy attached and I like the fact that unlike Yoga or T'ai Chi, it leaves me bone-tired, although in a totally exhilarating way.

Whenever anything happened in my life which made me feel disconnected or disoriented, I would go to more than my usual two exercise sessions a week. In the first few weeks after my brief encounter with Philip Anderway, I took class nearly every day. It paid off. I was able to sleep at night.

Despite seven hard-won hours of slumber, I tended to be irritable with Munch over little things, mostly her punctiliousness about the books. I avoided Alex altogether, even on the phone, and I indulged myself somewhat with customers.

Munch would have given me solace or hope or her two good ears. I wanted none of these from her. I accepted, grudgingly, her patience.

One morning, about three weeks after Philip Anderway entered and exited my life with Olympic speed, Mr. Shapley finally offered the price for the candlesticks that I had told Munch would consummate the sale.

I said no. Twenty-five dollars over that was my take-it-or-leave-it price. Instantly, as though he saw in my new implacability the tip of an iceberg he had best avoid meeting headlong, he caved in.

When he left the shop with the candlesticks a few minutes later, Mr. Shapley looked like a suitor accepted on terms he knew would very nearly ruin the match for him.

As the door clicked behind Mr. Shapley, I turned to Munch, prepared for an argument. Instead, she looked . . . hurt, and immediately returned to her work.

Not a word was said between us the remainder of the morning. Aside from that, it was quiet in the shop. We didn't have a single customer until shortly after noon, when a young man not more than nineteen or twenty came in to inquire about an amethyst ring in a window display of several pieces of antique jewelry.

The young man asked, with an old-fashioned formality, if he might see the ring. His shiny suit and narrow tie were as dated as his manners. He looked and sounded more like a character out of a nostalgic family television series than our usual customer.

I got the ring out of the window and laid it on a small velvet display stand. It was Victorian; the silver-work was fine; the amethyst small but good.

He didn't pick the ring up. He simply looked at it. I waited. I didn't say what a lovely little ring it was. As a matter of fact, I had been tempted to leave it out of the window display, toying with the idea of buying it myself. Finally, the young man looked up. "How much is it, ma'am?" he asked, his voice cracking with apprehension.

I said, "Eighty dollars," and heard a sharp intake

of breath from Munch's direction. But I knew she wouldn't say anything; we never differed in front of a customer, as though they were all children to whom it might be disquieting. "Is that within your range?" I asked him.

"Yes, ma'am, it is," the young man said, his pleasure undiluted by aplomb.

"Are you interested in it?" I asked in a tone which would have made Mr. Shapley quiver with gratification only hours earlier.

"Oh, I want it! Only," he hesitated, "I don't have the money on me. I do have it, though." I nodded reassuringly. "And I do have ten dollars on me. Would that do, as a deposit? I'd pick up the ring Saturday. Would that be satisfactory, ma'am?" There was sweat darkening the fine blond hairs on his upper lip.

"Certainly," I said.

He took out a plastic change purse that had seen newer—if not particularly better—days, removed a meticulously folded ten-dollar bill, smoothed it out, and presented it to me. I fetched a receipt book from Munch's desk, managing to avoid her eyes, and made out a receipt. "Your name?"

"Noah Gibbons."

I completed the receipt without smiling and handed it to him. "You won't sell it to anyone else?" Noah Gibbons asked.

"The ring is yours, Mr. Gibbons," I said. "You've put your money down on it."

"Right," he said. "Thank you. And I'll be here first thing Saturday morning."

"We don't open until ten." I said, envisioning what first thing might mean to Noah.

"Ten," he repeated. "Right. Goodbye now, ma'am. And thank you again."

"Thank you," I said.

Munch managed to contain herself until the door clicked behind Noah Gibbons. "Thank *you*," she said then in a fair imitation of my voice. "That ring cost us a hundred ten dollars."

I nodded. "And if you'd noticed them looking at it in the window last Saturday, you'd have given it to him for fifty dollars."

"That's what you think," said Munch.

"That's what I think," I said. "Besides, it was my decision and I'll cover the difference."

"The hell you will! Come on," Munch said, getting up from her desk and removing her purse from a drawer. "We're closing the shop for an hour and going to lunch at Le Veau d'Or. My treat."

"Closing the shop? During lunch hour?" I looked at the look on Munch and nodded. "Sure, why not. *Why?*"

"Because I'm entitled to feel good, too, lady," Munch said. "Besides, this is the first time in weeks I've seen you look pleased about anything. Whatever it was that was troubling you, you're over it now, aren't you?"

It took me a minute, but then I smiled. "You're right. I am." Sometime during that morning I seemed to have been drained of the last dregs of pain over Philip Anderway.

As we locked up and set off, enthusiastic as hooky players, I paused. "Munch, what would you say to my calling Mr. Shapley, when we get back from lunch, and saying I made a slight error when I quoted him our final price this morning?"

Munch regarded me with total seriousness. "It wouldn't be very businesslike."

"No."

"It might give him an edge next time."

"I don't think so," I said.

"I don't either," said Munch.

"So what do you say?"

"Welcome home."

6

"TAKE TOMORROW OFF and come shopping with me."

The call from Alex came late one Friday night, and there was a tautness in her voice that kept me from pointing out that we hadn't shopped together since Alex's freshman semester at Bennington; nor did I mention that Saturday was the day gallery hoppers along the avenue often stopped into the shop to browse, and sometimes to buy. Although Munch was perfectly capable of selling, that was generally conceded to be my province, and I was reluctant to leave Munch in the lurch to go *shopping*.

But I went.

Whether it was because of a maternal instinct that something was seriously wrong or just a maternal reflex, I went.

My first glance at Alex in the morning confirmed that clothes were not what was on her mind. Nonetheless, I followed in her wake through Bergdorf's, Bonwit's, Bendel's and Saks. Alex insisted on taking everything she bought, for which I was grateful, because eventually our arms and hands were totally occupied and Alex had to stop flinging her charge plates around, put down a few packages, and hail a taxi. We were closer to her place than mine; when she gave the driver my address, I knew the moment of truth, at least as Alex saw it, was approaching.

We piled out of the taxi with our bundles just in time to meet Charles Robinson and Raymond Elliott at the foot of the steps. The former was carrying two overflowing bags of food and some brown-bagged wine; the latter was carrying a big bundle of laundry and what must have been three bunches of daisies from the florist.

"Saturday in New York!" I said, verbally throwing up my hands.

"No one has any pocket money any more, yet the stores are full," said Charles Robinson. "The age of miracles isn't over."

"Mr. Robinson, Mr. Elliott, my daughter, Alexia Dobbs."

There was nodding all around. "Hi," said Raymond Elliott. "Sorry we can't be more neighborly and help you with some of those."

"I have my key out," Charles Robinson said, and so the four of us proceeded inside without further conversation.

Five minutes later, having dropped her bundles in the middle of my living room, Alex wandered over to the window and looked at some of my plants, a form of life in which she has not even cursory interest.

"Well now," I said, placing the packages I was carrying against a side wall and depositing myself on the sofa.

Alex turned to me. "Hi, there," she said in a poor imitation of Raymond Elliott's friendliness. "God!"

I found the disgust in her voice harsh and judgmental and really rather ugly. Still, she was upset; I was prepared to let it pass. "Alex, you wanted to talk to me about something?"

But Alex declined to change the subject so quickly. "Such domestic bliss! A communal laundry bag and heaps of daisies! You needn't look insulted. They're not friends of yours, are they?"

"No, they're not." It was a fact; so was my annoyance at my daughter.

"Well then," Alex's hands dismissed the subject at last.

Now we would get to it.

"Tell me," Alex said, "why do your plants grow so ferociously? Put this in my care for twenty-four hours"—she pointed to a creeping fig which responded with incredible grace to a bit of pampering—"and it would become terminal."

I was not prepared to argue the point; she was probably quite right. "I water them," I said.

"Everybody waters their plants."

Again I sidestepped disagreeing with her, although this time she was wrong. "I don't overwater them," I said.

"There's got to be more to it than that." The question period was over. She came over to the sofa, kicked off her Gucci loafers, and put her feet up on my coffee table. She looked around. "Too bad this place isn't a little bigger," she said, "I could move in with you."

No, my darling daughter, you could not. "I thought you came back here for more than a cup of Ching Wo tea."

"I don't want any tea," said Alex tonelessly, which was a tone I hadn't heard her take in a long time. What *was* wrong?

"That's what I was trying to say. A drink?"

"That wouldn't help."

"Can I?" asked her mother. After all.

Instantly, Alex's face seemed to fold in on itself as she lunged weeping into my unprepared arms. "Oh, Mama" was all she said for a time, between sieges of tears. I must admit I held her, at first, with a certain amount of reserve, because (I must also admit) I have reservations about my daughter. But then what I felt about her moved in on what I thought of her, and I held her tightly, until she was ready to talk.

Much later, when Alex had talked herself out, spewing forth an amazing number of details about an affair Tom had had, broken off, and confessed, in that order, I went into the kitchen to make a pot of tea for myself but more to leave Alex alone in the living room to make the telephone call she had decided, all by herself, without so much as a grunt of wisdom from me, to make.

I kept running the water, even after the kettle was filled, so I couldn't hear what she said. It couldn't have been very much, but apparently it was enough, or what Tom had replied was enough. In any case, it wasn't more than a few minutes before she appeared at the kitchen door, repairing her face in her compact mirror.

"Mom, I want to get home. Tom's waiting."

"Good," I said. "Go."

"You don't mind if I leave the packages until tomorrow? I mean, they won't be in your way? Actually, if I picked them up Monday before you left the house, I could take them directly to the stores and return them." She smiled. "I don't even remember what I bought."

"Sure. Leave them," I said. "Now, get going."

"Right," she said. I followed her to the door. "Mom? I love you," she said, and was gone.

I poured and drank my tea. There wasn't much alloy in that "I love you" of Alex's. She did love me, and she did love Tom, but she was a taker, not a giver. I could not shirk my responsibility for making her that way: in the years following Hal's death, I had tried to give her everything, and had come too close.

It must have been the sound of the ambulance stopping right under my windows which woke me.

Like most lifelong New Yorkers, I am, awake or asleep, immune to passing sounds.

I pulled my summer robe close and went over to the window. I looked down at the ambulance, then glanced at my watch. It was nearly two A.M. Behind me I heard the dialogue of an old reliable, a Bogart-Bacall film. It was nearly over. Agnes Morehead was making her last shrill denunciations; she was about to go out the window. I didn't have to turn toward the set; I knew what had happened, was happening, would happen.

Footsteps reached my landing. I waited for them to go on up, to old Mrs. Gobard, who insisted the fou1 flights of stairs were good exercise but who had to rest for minutes at each landing.

The steps didn't go on by. I moved to my door, but all I could hear were muffled voices and movements behind my neighbors' door. After a few minutes the door opened and feet receded down the stairs, very slowly.

I returned to the window. Two medics carrying a stretcher came out, followed by Charles Robinson, who climbed into the back of the ambulance after the stretcher was placed inside. In a moment the ambulance was gone. I hadn't even noticed the name of the hospital.

I turned off the set just as Bogart heard the music and turned to see Bacall in the doorway of the restaurant.

7

THERE WAS NO REASON I COULDN'T SLEEP LATE—it was Sunday morning—so I turned over. As I did, the half-open part of my half-closed eyes passed over the bedside clock, then reluctantly returned to it to verify that it was past noon. I had already slept late.

Then I remembered.

And was wide awake.

I got up, put coffee on to perk, threw on a shirt and pants and went out for the *Times*.

Later, after three cups of coffee (two more than I usually drink) and an unsuccessful swipe at the crossword puzzle, I busied myself with my plants, relieved to discover that two needed potting up. Roots were fighting their way out of all four drainage holes of my creeping fig; it was growing the way my hair tends to, confounding the answers-in-the-back-of-the-book. And a baby arrowhead I'd only had three weeks already sported half again as many leaves as when I'd bought it.

Good. I needed something to do. I spread the sports and financial sections on the floor and got out soil, vermiculite, a filled watering can, a knife and two pots, each a size bigger than its predecessor.

The repotting itself didn't take long; I had become expert at transferring a plant to a new home with operating-room concentration and minimum trauma. Inevitably, I made a mess, and cleaning that up, putting the stuff away and washing out the old pots took some time. Then I set the repotted plants gently aside where they'd be out of direct sunlight for a week.

I was misting the plants on the window sill when a taxi pulled up and Charles Robinson got out. He looked up at the house, and I hastily moved out of his sight-line. I waited for the sound of his step on the stairs, trying to decide if I had the nerve to open my door and ask how Raymond Elliott was, but there was no step on the stairs.

I went to the window, opened it, and leaned out. Yes. There he was, halfway up the block toward the park, walking slowly, his hands in his pockets, his head down. He looked sad, even from the back. But it was really none of my business. True, I liked both my next-door neighbors, but I didn't know either of them beyond exchanging amenities when we happened to meet. I *happened* to meet Raymond Elliott more frequently than Charles Robinson; also, he was more outgoing. All in all, I had no business intruding. Or, for that matter, staring at the receding figure of Charles Robinson.

I pulled my head back in.

"You hear the ambulance Saturday night?" Mrs. McPhee stopped sweeping the steps as I came outside, and leaned on her broom.

"Yes," I said, thinking I should move on. But I didn't; I waited.

But Mrs. McPhee knew when she had an important news item, and she waited, too.

"Do you happen to know how Mr. Elliott is?" I asked. "I mean, is he very sick?"

"Not no more," said Mrs. McPhee. "Just like babies," she added, shaking her head.

"Excuse me?"

"The middle of the night," she explained patiently. "He must have been dead by the time the ambulance reached the hospital."

She had to be wrong. "How do you *know*?"

"Saw 'im. I got responsibilities. I open my door when there's fuss-and-bother noises in the night. That was a dead face they carried out."

"I saw Mr. Robinson come back, but not to speak to," I said lamely. I felt glued to the step on which I stood.

"Nothin' to say," Mrs. McPhee sounded definitive.

"He was all right, you know, Mr. Elliott. A gorgeous dresser and always the gentleman. They both was that. You never heard them two quarreling. And they kept the place up nice, even made some improvements. With the landlord's written permission, of course. *That's* my business, the kind of tenants they were, if you know what I mean."

Oh, Alex, I thought, here's something for you: a cram course in tolerance. "Yes, Mrs. McPhee, thank you. Well, I really have to get to work—"

"Go on. But take my advice, take it easy. He was younger than you and me," said Mrs. McPhee.

Looking at her in the twice-sharp light of her comment and the morning, I realized for the first time that Mrs. McPhee was probably only a few years older than I. I had always taken her for a much older woman.

When I got to the shop, I busied myself rearranging a display case. I was feeling guilty: a little toward Mrs. McPhee for never really having looked at her before, but more toward Mr. Robinson because I had been so preoccupied with deciding what was or wasn't my business that it had never even occurred to me that Raymond Elliott might be sick enough to die of it.

Munch left me entirely alone for a couple of hours. But I must have been sending out signals for her to ask what the matter was.

"You rearranged that cabinet half an hour ago," she said. "Want to talk about it?"

"If I knew what there was to say . . ."

"Is it Alex and Tom again? I figured when she called to meet you on a Saturday—"

"They're all right. For now, anyway." I locked the cabinet and faced up to Munch. "Okay. The man next door died."

"The college teacher?"

"The other one. I think he was a set designer, I'm not sure. Munch, he couldn't have been more than thirty-five."

"That's rough," Munch said. "That's how old Hal was, thirty-five, wasn't he?"

"Thirty-four that June. I wonder if Mr. Robinson will move."

"Why would he? Rents being what they are . . ."

"It's hard to stay on, after. I moved."

"Yes, but that was different."

"They seemed . . . devoted."

"Okay, they were devoted. It's still different."

"You seem so sure," I said. *"How,* exactly?"

"They weren't *married.*"

"No," I said. "No, of course not."

Returning home from work that evening, my arms loaded with the week's grocery shopping, I expected to hear voices when I passed Charles Robinson's door, but there was no sound. I let myself into my apartment, not quite understanding. People must know by now.

Without much forethought I didn't turn on my stereo or the television. I spent the evening reading.

The next evening I got home a little later, because of my exercise class. When I reached the top of the stairs, I paused, deliberately listening. Again, no voices.

But there was sound: the sound of someone walking around at a broken pace, pausing continually, as if the person was stopping to look at things or to pick up something as he passed it. Suddenly, eavesdropping—the word—came to me. I hurried on to my own apartment.

That evening, again, I refrained from turning on music or television, although I had noticed in the *Times* a play on Channel 13 which sounded promising.

I *mended.*

What I was really doing was listening for arriving guests.

But no one came to see Mr. Robinson.

Wednesday evening I had a dinner date with Munch, her husband, Lew, and a customer of Lew's from out of town. He was a nice man—amiable, modestly interesting, not unlike Lew, and unattached. Dinner was pleasant. Herb Potter was obviously interested in me, but I felt increasingly edgy as dinner progressed, and when there was talk of going on to a supper club, I excused myself on the grounds of a headache, urged them to go on without me, and took a taxi home.

When I got there, I had no idea what to do with myself. I was somewhat annoyed. There had been no doubt that Herb Potter had taken my premature departure personally. I didn't think he would be calling me when next he came to New York. I wasn't sure I minded that, but neither was I sure why I had come home. Just to verify the silence next door? I minded *that; I* took *that* personally. But it had nothing to do with me, and there was nothing I could do about it.

I picked up a Doris Lessing paperback I had been saving for a rainy weekend. I like her work.

When I found myself reading the same page for the fourth time, I knew it had nothing to do with the book.

My mind kept pushing me somewhere else. I closed the book, and my eyes, and gave in to it.

A chiaroscuro scene. At the center is a young woman with a familiar face. She is surrounded by other women and men. Behind a buffet table stand two older women in dressy black dresses shielded by aprons. One of the women fills a plate with food and brings it to the woman around whom everyone is clustered, but she shakes her head. The woman stands there, apparently insisting, for a moment, then she goes away. People keep coming up to the central figure and taking her hands. Many of them kiss her, she receives it all, but nothing seems to come from her. I look closer, at her chest. She is breathing shallow, slow breaths. I look at her face, pale, drawn, a much younger me. She looks terrible, waxen, that me; I want to look away, but I cannot.

Suddenly, footsteps coming up the stairs. *Not* then— now.

I brushed a tear from my cheek. No one must see me like this. Silly woman. They weren't coming to my apartment, but to Charles Robinson's. Finally.

But the steps continued past my door and on upstairs.

There was no way to hold them back then. The tears, cutting as shards of March rain, hit my cheeks and arms. I did not try to stanch them. I just let them come and come—tears for the solitary mourning of the stranger next door; tears stored inside me for a decade, because all those people who had come when Hal had died had not been able to fill that room.

When the tears stopped, I fell asleep. I slept all night like that, curled into a corner of the sofa.

First thing the following morning I sold an Edwardian tea service and two large candelabra to a modestly dressed woman. When the door clicked behind the woman, Munch said, "Appearances are deceiving. Are yours?"

"It was a nice sale," I said. "The August rent and a bit more."

"Annie, what's up?"

No one calls me Annie. Except Munch, very rarely, as a loving shorthand for *please, can I help?*

I sighed. "You ought to get those new glasses of yours checked."

"They're that good, huh?"

"I'm afraid so. All right. It's that—remember, when Hal died, how many people came? You and Lew were at the house every night for a week."

"Sure. What are friends for?"

"For *that*, for one thing. I don't think a single person has come to see Mr. Robinson."

"That's a shame," Munch said, meaning it. "Still, it's understandable, isn't it?"

No. No, it's not. I don't understand it. "Yah," I said. "I suppose so."

.   .   .

I cut my exercise class; by evening, the night spent on the couch had gotten to me. I went directly home, took a shower, and went to bed with a bowl of vichyssoise and Doris Lessing. At seven-thirty I got up out of bed and rearranged my tiny, neat linen closet. That accomplished nothing: the closet was just as neat, in differently ordered piles, and I was just as tense as when I started.

I needed more radical treatment. I decided to clean my oven. Like listening to a recording of Lee Wiley singing "My Funny Valentine," it was a sure thing.

Nearly always.

It did help. Some.

Afterward, lying in an oil-fragrant tub, the most foolproof relaxant I know, I could still feel the coils in my back as I leaned against the curved porcelain. I deliberately put Mr. Robinson out of my mind. I put everything out of my mind. I concentrated on the balletic grace of my Boston fern, hanging beneath a special spotlight attached to the wall above its bracket. As the steam from the tub rose, the fern seemed to move within it. Like a cinder, into my mind's eye flew the picture of all the flowers that had come when Hal died, and how they had smelled to me, until they could decently be thrown out, of his dying. Because flowers, once cut, are themselves dying.

Then, unwittingly, unwillingly, I see myself sitting on a straight-backed chair, my eyes red but dry, looking up at Hal's boss, who is looking down at me reassuringly. Then Munch approaches, holding a plate of food. I shake my head, but she sits down beside me, giving Hal's boss the reason he needs to excuse himself, and she feeds me finger food with her fingers—lovingly, slowly, patiently, as though I am a sick child. And then she feeds me tea with a spoon, until I have finished half a cup. I find that eating has not revived me, but instead has exhausted me. I don't tell Munch, or anyone, and they stay. I am not sorry; I want them there. I do not want to be alone.

I got out of the tub and made myself a pot of Jasmine Blossom tea, a favorite of mine. It was a mistake, because I drank two cups and when I finally returned to bed at half past eleven I still couldn't get to sleep.

The next morning Munch left me alone. She didn't ask why I looked so tired, she knew. At our age, when you don't get a good night's sleep, you don't look good. Nor did she ask me why I hadn't slept. I did hardly anything and not one customer came in the entire day.

Beside me, a half-eaten salad sat wilting in the humid air. I had the stereo on low, having decided that not playing it might become conspicuous. It was a late Beethoven quartet, a somber piece, which suited my mood.

Tired as I was, I knew that if I went to bed I would only lie there. I have had sporadic insomnia all my life and I can usually tell in advance when going to bed, even with a glass of warm milk and honey, would be pointless.

I leaned back against the sofa pillows and listened to the sad music Beethoven had heard only in his head.

I heard crying. For a second I thought it came from next door.

But then I knew it wasn't Charles Robinson I heard, but Alex, crying—years ago—the way a child cries whose father has just died.

I go into her room. I constantly feel guilty toward her these past weeks. After all, she has lost her father, but I cannot seem to focus on her and her pain at all. I know she has been feeling pain; it has been visible in her dry eyes. Until tonight she hasn't cried.

She wants to know the truth, she tells me. What did she do that made Daddy go away? I tell her—Nothing, she has done nothing wrong. He just had a heart attack. It happens. She had nothing to do with it. But she doesn't believe me. She thinks that grownups always have a choice: that is the difference between being a child and being grown-up. If he had a heart attack, it was on purpose. To leave her. To punish her. She is wrong, I tell her. Sometimes grownups have to do things too: Daddy had to die. And then she tells me; she can no longer hold it in. I'm wrong. She knows why Daddy died.

Blurting out her shame between streams of tears, she tells me that the week before Hal died, she stole fifty cents from where he always left his change on our dresser.

Poor, poor Alex.

For the first time I can share her grief, and we hold each other and cry. I tell her that she is a good little girl, that all little girls, even ones as good as she is, do something bad sometimes.

Instantly, she stops crying and asks me what I did, when I was her age, that was as bad as what she has done. I cannot think of anything; I assure her that I did plenty of things, I just cannot remember one right now. But she insists that if I am right, if she is not to blame for her Daddy's dying, then I have to prove it by remembering some terrible deed of mine—because both my parents are still alive.

And then I remember.

I tell her that when I was nine my brother, her Uncle Pete, who was ten then, wet his bed. I told his best friend. Alex looks at me with her enormous brown eyes, considering. That was bad, she says, but was it as bad as stealing fifty whole cents from Daddy? Neither one was really very bad, I say, just not a good thing to do. But was it *as* bad? she persists. Yes, I say, it was as bad. And, in a second, she is asleep in my arms.

I wait a few minutes, but she is sleeping soundly, a half-smile on her face. I settle her, and go back into the living room.

Even though it is past midnight, I call Munch and I tell her, and she tells me something she did when she was ten and for a week waited for the sky to fall, and then we laugh. She says, You sound . . . almost like you.

I'll live, I say. Good night now.

I sit for a while before I go to bed, glad that I have been able to give Alex something for the first time since Hal died: an old, secret sin of mine to cut hers down to size. And Munch has given me a reason to laugh again.

Yes, when someone dies, you live, so long as there's someone around to remind you not to feel guilty because you're alive, breathing, doing good things and not so good things, being . . . being alive. You need someone to remind you that you're still alive not simply by default.

And that you've still got choices to make.

I sat up straight then, knowing what I must do.

I went into my kitchen, got out mixing bowls, pans, spatulas, sifter, mixer, eggs, butter, vanilla, chocolate— everything needed to bake a cake. I glanced at the kitchen clock. It was eight-forty. I set to work.

Later, while the cake cooled in front of the air conditioner, I dressed and made up my face. Rejecting my customary pants suits for a simple green linen dress, I added a handsome Moroccan enamel pin to the neckline. Then I iced the cake, steadied it on a large plate, grabbed my keys, and went.

Outside his door, I hesitated for the merest moment, took a deep breath, and rang the bell. Steps came toward the door and stopped.

"Who is it?" asked Mr. Robinson's voice from inside.

"It's Anne Durham, Mr. Robinson." There was silence from inside. "From next door," I added, just to dull it.

Another, briefer silence. Then the door opened. Mr. Robinson, wearing a shirt open at the neck and looking as if he had not slept in days, stood peering at me, obviously at a loss to know why I had rung his bell for the first time in the two years we had lived in neighboring apartments.

Then he glanced down, saw the cake, looked back at my face, and stepped aside, opening the door wide. Wordlessly, he motioned me to enter.

"I know it's late to call," I said, as though I were someone who occasionally did call but at a more conventional hour. I placed the cake on a table.

"Won't you sit down," he said, taking a jacket off the back of a chair and putting it on.

I sat in the nearest chair. Charles Robinson nodded as if something had been accomplished. Then he walked over to the table on which I had placed the cake and looked at it. "It's a beautiful cake," he said. "You really shouldn't have gone to all that trou—" He stopped himself, turned, and looked at me. "Thank you."

"It's chocolate," I said, and I suppose I've said a stupider thing in my life, sometime.

"It looks delicious," he said, looking at it again. Then, turning to me once more, he said, in a slightly raised voice as if projecting from a stage, "Would you like a cup of coffee with it?"

It hadn't occurred to me that we would eat the cake. And I never drink coffee except at breakfast. But the look on his face, a face I had seen once on a tightrope walker, swayed me. "If you have any tea . . . ?"

"Better still," said Mr. Robinson. "I'm not much of a coffee drinker myself. I won't be long." He headed for the kitchen. In a moment he was back, and smiling apologetically for the oversight, got the cake.

I looked around. It's funny, when you live next door to people you never really think about what their apartment might look like, but if you ever do see it, you realize that you had a picture in mind anyway. Mine had been wrong. I had conjured up a room that was all of a piece—rather chic. I suppose I thought it would look more *done*, because I had gathered Raymond Elliott was a set designer. Instead, it was obviously a room that had "happened" over a period of years. There was a leather sofa, a wing chair covered in a dull print, a pair of good French chairs covered in worn teal velvet, an assortment of tables (two modern glass-and-chrome, the rest dark woods) and, on the tables, clusters of photographs in silver frames. They appeared to be family pictures: a number of people of different generations bearing some family resemblance. The picture closest to me was of a stunning young girl in a cap and gown. High school graduation? College? I couldn't tell. A sign of how old I myself was getting.

Mr. Robinson returned carrying a tray on which a pot of tea, cups and saucers and the appropriate ac-couterments, and two large slices of cake on lovely dishes clattered from the unsteadiness of his hands. He set the tray down carefully and poured the tea. "How do you take it?"

"Black," I said, and took the rose, green and white Limoges cup and saucer he handed me. "Such pretty children," I said as he handed me one of the cake plates. "Thank you."

"Yes. They . . . they're mostly Raymond's nieces and nephews. He came from a large family."

I inclined my head toward the picture of the girl in commencement dress. "She's a beauty."

"Merilee, yes. She's a sophomore at Holyoke."

"Is she as mischievous behind those fine features as she looks?"

Mr. Robinson looked at the picture a moment, then nodded. "I see what you mean," he said.

Just-poured tea is always too hot for me. Now I took a sip of it. "Lapsang Soochang," I noted with pleasure. "How very nice."

Mr. Robinson said, "I never met her."

With some effort I did not look away. "I'm sorry," I said, trying not to make too much of it.

"I am too," he said. "She was a favorite of Raymond's." He took a bite of the cake. "It's delicious," he said. "It was really very kind of you."

"I don't bake often. It's too mathematical for me. But that recipe came from my mother's mother. It is special."

"It's delicious."

"Do they live far away?" I said, getting off the cake.

"I'm sorry?"

"Mr. Elliott's family. I mean . . ." My hand swept the room, taking in the dozens of photographs. "They're so many of them, yet no one's come." The moment it was out of my mouth I would have done anything to retrieve it.

"Oh," said Mr. Robinson after a moment, "I see. Well, they're kind of scattered. His mother lives in Charleston." A pause. "She came." A longer pause. Then, quietly, looking somewhere past my left shoulder, "I called her from the hospital. It was all over already. It was all over so fast. She flew up"—his voice faltered, but only for the second it took me to wish I were dead—"and claimed his body."

He was in control of his voice now; his hands had even stopped shaking. "The funeral was yesterday."

Propelled by shock, I said, "You didn't go?"

"The funeral was in Charleston, Mrs. Durham." Then, gently, "It was a private service for the family only." He took another bite of the cake and another sip of tea. "It was really good of you to bake this. You really shouldn't have gone to so much . . ." His voice trailed off. He looked at me.

"Should I go?"

Without an iota of impoliteness in the gesture, Mr. Robinson shrugged. He really didn't know if I should go. I didn't either. What to do, what would be best to do, what to do which would be *least harmful*—indecision filled the room like smoke. Finally, in no more than a terribly elongated moment, he said, "I'm sorry."

"*You're* sorry. Dear God!" I put down the teacup and stood. Automatically, Mr. Robinson stood too. I went to the door; that close to leaving, I had to say *something*.

"Mr. Robinson, eleven years ago my husband died. I had a young daughter—you met her the other day—she was only eleven then . . ."

"It must have been very difficult for you," he said, genuine sympathy in his voice.

"Yes. And yet, you see, people came—"

"You're very kind," Mr. Robinson said.

"What I am, Mr. Robinson, is a woman who has blundered in here without thinking what I might say to you, and I've managed to say all the wrong things. Mr. Robinson, I'm terribly sorry your friend is dead."

Before he could say a word, I was out the door. I rushed to my own apartment and let myself in quickly. But I needn't have hurried so.

There was no sound of a door opening behind me.

8

"THAT LIPSTICK'S NICE ON YOU."

Munch looked up at me over her eyeglasses. "Thanks," she said. "I've thought so ever since I got it, back last winter."

"Sorry."

"Look, as long as you don't remark on my perfume, which I've been using since we were both eighteen, you're home free."

"What's it called?"

Munch looked at the bottom of the lipstick case. "Sunbathed Red," she said evenly. "You're really interested in lipsticks this morning."

"I paid a condolence call on Mr. Robinson last night."

Munch blotted her lips. Twice. "You really went and visited him?"

I nodded. "I baked him a cake."

"You're kidding." Munch looked at me. "You're not kidding. What kind?"

"My grandmother's chocolate. Is that really what you want to know?"

"I can't help it if I don't know what to ask. What did he say?"

"He said it was delicious."

"You ate it?"

"He made us tea."

"But what did he *say*?"

"Not much. He was very polite. Gracious, really. I guess he was surprised."

"That makes two of us."

"Three."

"Well, go on, tell me. What did *you* say?"

"Not very much. I just felt I had to do it. I mean, *no one* came. Once I was there, I didn't know what to say. It's not as though I know him. At least, with Raymond Elliott, we used to bump into each other a lot. I guess we kept more or less the same morning schedule. Not that I knew him, either. Munch, he made tea and we ate a piece of cake and I said a few dumb things and then, as I was leaving, I just blurted out how sorry I was. I really botched it."

"Look, lady, I don't pretend to understand why you went. But since you went, I'm sure whatever you said was the right thing. You're good at that."

"Condolence calls?"

"No. Finding words. Tell me, what's the apartment like?"

"Nice. Warm. A lot of books. A lot of photographs."

"*Special* ones?"

"What did you have in mind?"

Munch retreated immediately. "*I* don't know." But it was not a full retreat and I closed in on her . . . tiptoeing.

"No, nothing special in the way of pictures. His whip collection was pretty impressive."

"His what?" Munch gasped. She is not the least gullible of women.

"Whips," I said, swooshing my arm through the air in illustration. "Dozens of them. In a corner cabinet. Sort of like the mahogany one you keep your mother's Royal Doulton in."

Munch caught on at last; she also caught a whopping

case of offendedness. "I don't think I like your making fun of me."

"The alternative, my dear Munch," I said in a somewhat conciliatory voice, feeling I had perhaps gone a bit far, "was to take you over my knee and spank you. What if a customer had walked in?"

"You're very . . . sophisticated about the whole thing."

"Not *very*. From what I can remember about what I said last night, I sounded anything *but* sophisticated. Look, all I *know* is, that man who died was a nice man. And Mr. Robinson, he's a nice man." I looked to see if I was getting through to Munch. I saw no sign of recognition. "They were decent human beings. I was trying to do a decent thing. That's *all!*"

"Anne, we're fighting." Munch's voice was clogged with held-back tears.

I took a beat to calm down. "We were," I said. After a shorter beat, "It's just that somebody lost somebody. And there's nothing sophisticated about *that.*"

Munch took off her glasses. "No, I guess there isn't," she said.

9

SO CAREFULLY WAS I CARRYING THE GRACEFUL grey-green crassula that had caught my eye on my way past the plant store on the corner that I nearly tripped over the cake plate tilted against my door. Glancing down, I saw, in addition to the plate, a slim package wrapped in silver paper. I put down the plant, set aside the plate and package, and let myself into the apartment.

A few minutes later, having placed the crassula in a sunny spot on my window sill and given it a few words of welcome, I sat down on the sofa and opened the note Scotch-taped to the package. In a rather large hand, in brown pen, it said: "Raymond and I each had a copy of this. I want you to have his. Sincerely, Charles Robinson."

I laid the note aside and unwrapped the package. Between two pieces of corrugated cardboard, in a plain brown dust jacket, was a single 78 record. I got up, placed the record on the turntable, reset the needle, and put it on very low.

Dropping to the rug, I listened four times through to the old, incredibly exquisite Alex Schiøtz recording of the Buxtehude "Aperite."

10

I REJECTED THE IDEA OF REPLYING to Charles Robinson's note with a thank-you note of my own. I wanted to tell him in person that the Buxtehude cantata was among my most vividly remembered early musical experiences.

I had first heard it on a Saturday afternoon when I was thirteen at the apartment of a girl who was my best friend and, being a year older than I, my mentor as well. She had introduced me to Guerlain's Mitsouko and the subtleties of Claire McCardell clothes, which, if I could not afford to wear them, I could at least gape over. My friend Glorya actually owned a mud-mauve McCardell!

She was wise beyond her years, which she proved for the twentieth time that day when I arrived at her door the victim of a five-block war on my nerves. Walking to Glorya's house through an astonishingly fierce rain, I had passed a woman kneeling in a doorway on Central Park West, crying out loud to God for cessation of his wrath, and that had scared me more than the piercing rain. Glorya took one look at me, ordered me to remove all my clothes, and wrapped me in her floor-length putty flannel bathrobe. I continued to tremble.

What I needed, she announced, was a strong dose of serenity, and left the room. I expected her to come back with a cup of hot chocolate or, given Glorya's sophistication, one of her mother's pills or even some of her father's brandy. What she came back with was a record of the Buxtehude cantata, the same 78 recording Charles Robinson later gave me. She played it for me over and over; and of course it worked. Glorya always knew what to do.

Afterward, when I was calm, we discussed the merits and demerits of certain names, and agonizing over the final contenders, settled on Carla and Ethan as the best of all possible names for our future, best-friends children. I cannot remember if we were each to have a Carla and an Ethan or divide the spoils between us; as it turned out, Hal chose Alexia, and Glorya had an emergency hysterectomy at nineteen.

I kept expecting to run into Charles Robinson, but an entire week passed without our meeting. By Friday evening I regretted not having slipped a note under his door; he would think me rude. But I was tired and had a long Saturday in front of me; I would do something about rectifying the situation the first chance I got.

Saturday morning my alarm went off at five, and by seven I was strapped into my seat on a flight to Chicago. I went directly from the airport to the gallery where a large estate auction which included a number of remarkable silver pieces was taking place.

By three-thirty the auction was over. I had bid on five items. On three I was outbid, one by a clean thousand dollars; of the two items on which I had bid successfully, one was spectacularly beautiful and the other I got for a hundred and fifty dollars less than my top bid.

By four-twenty I had paid for my purchases and arranged for them to be delivered to me on the airplane by insured messenger.

By four-forty I was at the Art Institute, with just enough time to enjoy the two magnificent Blue Period Picassos and the two El Grecos which were my favorite paintings there, before the museum closed and I had to grab a cab for the airport anyway.

Remembering that I hadn't had lunch, I grabbed

a bittersweet chocolate bar at an airport newsstand and made my plane with ten minutes to spare.

The aircraft was already crowded, however, and I had to settle for an aisle seat toward the back.

During takeoff (a moment I never miss) I had to strain past the man seated in the window seat to see out. Becoming airborne gives me thoroughgoing pleasure every time. To me, being afraid of flying is a little like being unsusceptible to sunsets: it arouses my sympathy but not an iota of empathy.

We were flying.

I sat back, ate my chocolate bar, and thought about what a profitable day it had been: two good purchases, four great paintings. Altogether a worthwhile trip.

"A drink, ma'am?" I had drifted off. A stewardess was leaning over me. I hesitated.

"May I buy you a drink?" I turned to the voice. It belonged to the man in the window seat, a man my age, perhaps a couple of years younger, an edge too conventionally good-looking for my taste.

"No, thank you," I said to the man. "No, thank you," I said to the stewardess.

"I'll have a Dewar's, please," the man said to the stewardess. "You're sure?" he said to me.

I nodded. The stewardess served him his drink and passed on.

"You don't drink?" he said.

I was annoyed. Why didn't he just leave it?

I have never considered juxtaposition on an airplane a good enough reason for conversation. Concerts, the theatre, sometimes. But in an airplane, the proximity is too artificially intimate. Besides, if the stranger beside you turns out to be truly strange or, even worse, demandingly boring, where can you go? How many trips to the lavatory can you make on a plane trip without succumbing to instant acute claustrophobia. Stop it before it starts is my airborne motto.

"I don't drink alone," I said. Social fencing isn't a sport I especially enjoy, but I can parry deftly enough when I have to.

"I see," he said, and drank his drink alone. I closed my eyes again. I felt rather pleased with my retort: succinct, severe, successful. I indulged in alliterative self-congratulation.

And snide.

"If I asked you to have dinner with me this evening, would you say you don't eat alone?"

I opened my eyes and turned my head toward him. No, it wasn't an interesting face. But if you do try to keep your prejudices in line, how can you really hold it against him that his features are even? Besides, he had guts. There seemed little likelihood that he would turn out to be either notably strange or notably boring.

"All right," I said.

"You'll have dinner with me?" He sounded *happy*.

"I'll have a conversation with you," I said. I smiled, to take the edge off my compromise.

"Good!" he said. Still happy. Cocky? Or easy to please?

"Why?"

"Why not?" he said.

"I meant, why did you offer me a drink? Dinner? Et cetera?"

"Et cetera?" he repeated.

I waited.

"Because I find women who like to fly and who dare

to eat a chocolate bar very nearly irresistible," he said lightly.

Cocky, I decided. "My! My mother never told me it would be this easy."

"Neither did mine," he said quietly.

"I don't think it is, actually," I said. The last word.

"I didn't think it was, actually," he said, having it after all, but without any satisfaction in his voice.

I picked up the airline's magazine, stuck in the rack in front of me. In ten minutes I had read it from cover to cover.

Why was I so bloody indignant? Because he found me attractive? I wore make-up; I washed my hair every morning; I wore well-fitting clothes in unmurky colors. I was attractive. I meant to be. Besides, would I like it thrown up to me when I found a *man* attractive?

I closed the magazine. Why not?

"Why not?" I said to him. "My name is Anne Durham. I'm a New Yorker. I run a small shop specializing in antique silver. I've been in Chicago to attend an estate auction." I checked—he wasn't caressing me with his eyes, he was listening. My mind went blank. His eyes were an off-beat brown. Off-beat brown? A real brown. Warm. Like mink in the old days. "I went to P.S. 173," I said.

"I wish I had," he said, all seriousness. Then he smiled for the first time, and it happened sideways. It sort of slipped across his face, taking just long enough to reveal a space between his two front teeth, and then was gone. That smile ameliorated the conventionality of his looks. He was really quite attractive, I decided.

"Thank you, Anne Durham. I'm David. Meray. I was born in Atlanta, but I live in Chicago. I'm an architectural consultant." His eyes flickered briefly with uncertainty. "And I get to New York for a few days about once a month."

That uncertainty, it piqued my interest. Then it scared me. Who asked you how often you get to New York? I didn't tell you that I get to Chicago once a year, maybe less often. Did I indicate in any way that I might be interested in how often you come to New York?

"Your trip to Chicago," he broke the silence when I wouldn't, "that's not a regular thing, is it? I mean, there wouldn't be that many estate auctions worth coming a thousand miles for, would there?"

"Hardly," I said, chiseling the word out of marble. "The last time I was in Chicago was in 1953." The lie came out smoothly. I smoothed my lips down over it like crepe over narrow hips; it fit fine.

"My husband was stationed at Chanute Field." That much was true. Hal was not, after all, my ex-husband or my former husband. One would not be required, by etiquette (or kindness?), to say my dead husband. My husband who passed away eleven years ago. My husband. That's how you get him, Mister David Meray. "I especially wanted to get to the Art Institute after all this time," I said.

"Picasso's guitarist," he said, ignoring the rest.

Don't ignore my husband. You may not dismiss him that peremptorily from this conversation. From the world.

"My husband's favorite," I said, lying.

In fact, Hal had felt about museums much the way most people feel about cemeteries, not a nice place to visit at all.

But *I love* that painting.

74

I am lying too much; I will shortly begin to deceive us both. "It's a very good museum," I said.

There.

"For the Midwest?" The smile slanted; the voice arched. Then: "Sorry. You didn't mean it that way, did you? Look, if I'm being defensive, it's because I'm afraid you'll turn me down. Don't. Please. Have dinner with me tonight."

"How," I asked, my voice on a leash held tight, "do you know I'm not married?"

"A guess," he said. "Only a guess. You're not, are you? Not now, I mean?"

"No," I said, inexplicably annoyed, "I'm not married now."

But you are. I just knew.

It takes two to tango but only one to commit adultery, so to speak. Your wife— Where is she? Where are we?

"But you are," I said, saying it out loud but not too loud, for both of us to hear but no one else. My cards are the only ones on the table—we are short some cards, my friend.

Silence—the longest minute. I looked at my nails. Neatness counts. They were neatly manicured, cut relatively close but not too close. Too close. I wriggled in my seat, trying to get some distance from the situation, trying to find a comfortable position. There wasn't any.

"Yes," he said finally, "I am. If you'll still have dinner with me, I'll tell you about it."

I shook my head.

"That's it?" he said, and having misunderstood me, sounded really very disappointed.

"No, I'll have dinner with you," I told him. "But there is a condition."

He looked at me and waited.

I will have dinner with you but not with her.

"The condition is that you don't tell me about it. All right?"

It was, obviously, not the condition he expected. He looked surprised, as if he'd offered me a package and I'd declined to open it. Aren't you even curious? his eyes asked. His mouth said, "Of course, if that's how you want it. Of course."

11

DAVID MERAY AND I SHARED A TAXI as far as my apartment. Then he took it on downtown to his hotel. He would pick me up in an hour.

At the foot of the steps of the house, I met Charles Robinson coming down. There was a young man with him who wore pale-grey knitted trousers and a silky maroon shirt open nearly to the waist. Around his neck he wore a gold chain, suspended from which was a cross, a c'hai and a Buddhist long-life symbol. Mr. Robinson wore a slightly embarrassed expression.

It was I who should be embarrassed. "Hello," I said. "I've been hoping to run into you."

"Hello," he said.

"It's drizzling," the young man said.

This obviously wasn't the time to discuss Buxtehude.

"It's beginning to rain. I won't keep you now." I started up the steps.

"Cab . . . cab!" I heard the young man's voice call out. "Damn! It went by!"

"It's only around the corner," Mr. Robinson said in a placating voice.

"We *need* a taxi. I *won't* get wet."

I reached the top of the stairs and pushed the outer door open.

"All right," I heard Mr. Robinson say as the door closed behind me, "we'll take a taxi."

I heard the phone ringing, dashed out soap-covered, and answered. "Hello!"

"Hi!" It was Munch. "You sound out of breath. Did you just get in?"

"Five minutes ago. I'm soaking wet, Munch."

"It's only drizzling."

"I'm in the shower."

"Oh, sorry! I'll call back in fifteen minutes."

"Can't. I have to get ready. Going out to dinner."

"You haven't got anything at all in the house?"

"I didn't say that." I laughed.

"Oh! You met someone on the plane. Fantastic! What's he like?"

"Not fanatically prompt, I hope. Munch, does my cream silk still look pretty terrific?"

"That nice, huh? It looks sensational. I can't wait to tell Lew."

"Yes you *can*. Please?"

"Okay. Sure. I'll call you in the morning."

"I'll call *you* in the morning."

"Have a marvelous time!"

"Thanks, Munch. Munch?"

"Uh huh?"

"Thanks."

"Are you angry because I broke my word?"

"No," I said. I was not angry. I was . . . indignant.

"Then?"

Then what? He wanted to know. I'd like to know myself.

All right. Let's find out. Sometimes, when someone asks me a question, I have to find the answer through giving it: the thoughts and words come in tandem. I struggled for them now; they seemed just out of reach. I stretched.

"I think," I began, trying, "I think that we can be merciless to ourselves, and that that's as bad as being merciless to someone else. Do you really think," I said, "that it's made a difference to your son, that you stayed together? He isn't even home. Does he even know?"

"I did what seemed right at the time." He spoke undefensively. "Can you understand that?" There was no challenge in his voice; he expected me to understand.

"Yes, it's easy to see. Still . . ." I paused, not sure I wanted to follow my train of thought. Then I did want to. "You were separated for nearly a year, and then because once—from habit, from loneliness, from any one of a dozen reasons neither good nor bad but *there*—you happened into bed together and a child was

conceived. This retarded young man . . . this *always* child.
You decided to stay until she gave birth; decency dictated
it. But when the baby was . . . not right, you arbitrarily
extended your self-inflicted nine-months' sentence to
life?"

"It hasn't been *prison.*" Now he did sound defensive.
Small wonder. Sometimes my way with words got away
from me. "Alice—my wife—is not a terrible person.
We've managed. We take care to respect the bounds."

I was suddenly angry. "The bounds of matrimony!
Oh, David!"

Then he was as angry as I. "Your marriage was
perfect?"

I looked at him, startled. And thought back to Hal.
The light of memory tends to be, like the light in a
good restaurant, romantically dim. I strained to see
clearly. "No," I said, "my marriage was not perfect."
There.

No. I was intrigued. I tried to remember it: my
marriage.

I remembered a blue velvet dress I'd had when I
was seven. There was an ecru lace collar, a pilgrim collar.
I could see me in it as clearly as in a freshly cleaned
mirror. But my marriage. I tried to see me in that. I
did try.

After a time I said, "No, of course it wasn't perfect.
But it was real—it was something we had, and did, and
were . . . together." It sounded wonderful. I felt tears
rising, and had a moment of schizophrenia. I felt certain
that the tears in my right eye were there because my
description of my marriage was true, and the tears in
my left eye were there because it was not as true as I
made it sound, even to me.

I wanted to tell him that—and to have him hold me and say it was all right. But I couldn't. I barely knew him, anyway—what had gotten into me?

David, to spare me and/or himself embarrassment, looked away and signaled the waiter for our check, while I blotted both my true and my false eye with my napkin.

When the taxi reached my house, David did hesitate, at least perfunctorily. I told him to let it go and come on up for a brandy. I wasn't sure about asking him up, but something in me didn't want him to leave yet.

I got the brandy and the snifters, and while he poured, I put the Buxtehude "Aperite" on the stereo.

When the piece ended, David turned to me, his eyebrows furrowed.

"You didn't like it," I said.

"Is this a test?" he asked. His voice was even.

"Of course not," I said in all truth. I *wanted* him to like it, but it was not a requirement and I was disappointed he might think I had tests to give. I wasn't at all sure what I did have to give—or what I wanted from him—but tests had nothing to do with it.

His eyebrows resumed their normal spacing. "I liked it," he said.

I was glad; I put my disappointment in its place. "Oh, good," I said, "it has such a rare serenity—"

"That eluded me." He got up and began to walk around the room, as if stalking some answer. Finally, he came to a halt before the window. He stood with his back to me, looking out. "Serene is the very opposite of how I feel right now."

I watched his back; it was very straight. He was taller than I'd realized, at least an inch over six feet.

"You make me feel like a boy, awkward and hesitant.

And I don't like it. I want to kiss you, hold you. I want you. I don't like being made to feel like a boy who doesn't know how to behave—what is acceptable, what will cause me to be sent from the room . . ."

He stopped speaking but did not turn around. I got up and stood behind him. I wanted to touch his back. I didn't.

"I can't even turn around and say it to your face," he said, but he was looking at my face reflected in the window. Then he did turn around and look down at me, and he looked very serious—not at all like a boy, and yet vulnerable. I raised up on my toes and he bent downward and we kissed. I was surprised at it, at myself, at how much I wanted, at how urgently I wanted it.

I broke away. I moved away. I touched the leaves of my dieffenbachia, tall and straight, the way he was.

Look, touch, but do not chew, I remembered the dieffenbachia is poisonous if eaten. Do not expose young children to its dangers, they are susceptible.

So are forty-three-year-old women.

"Just like that," David said, and then cleared his throat.

In the silence before I said anything, I could hear my own breathing and his, although I had moved several feet away. I felt, as I had on the plane, too great an intimacy being forced on me. "That's the point," I said. "Not just like that."

"You came to me. You *came* to me."

"Oh, yes," I said, unable even to try to defend myself against that bald fact.

"No matter how much you loved him, he's dead, Anne."

For a fraction of a second I had no idea whom

he meant. Then, of course. "Hal? He's been dead a long time, David. He's not standing between us."

"Then what is it!"

I sought the word. "Demography?" I suggested finally. It was not exactly right, but it was the best I could do.

"Demography," he repeated, as if in a spelling bee. "Demography," he said again, this time as though deciding if it suited him, if he would *take* it. "Meaning that certain Chicagoans are married."

I nodded. The word would do.

I looked at the remarkably self-sufficient dieffenbachia. It looked suddenly as though it needed misting. I resisted reaching for the mister on the table behind me.

"What was that kiss about, then? I'm a little old for spin-the-bottle."

I winced. "It wasn't a game," I said. "It was about . . . feeling."

"Just not enough feeling to go any further?" He sounded like a boy again. Hurt. Angry. Confused. He must hate the way he sounds.

All right. Maybe I owed it to him. Maybe everybody owed everybody the truth. "I'm scared," I said.

It took a moment for that to reach him and then no time at all for him to reach out, move to me, embrace me. I responded. *Again.* And then *again*, I disengaged myself—gently, as gently as any act so essentially ungentle can be. "David, I like you. I also like myself. Too much to get involved with a man who is . . . otherwise involved."

"I've been absolutely honest with you!"

"Honesty is no excuse." I nearly whispered it, but he looked as if I'd slapped him. Obviously, until this occasion, honesty about his marriage had stood him in good stead, so to speak. He looked not only hurt but surprised.

"Perhaps," I said, "I should not have gone to dinner with you. But, well, dinner—there's nothing decisive about dinner in a restaurant. But when you held me— all right, when *we* kissed—that was real. Real enough to remind me that I'm not up to all the realities of a love affair with a married man." It sounded like a fifties lyric; still, it was true. "I haven't the stamina."

"You seem to have a flair for coming to conclusions swiftly. About my marriage. Now, about us."

"I have an articulate gut," I said, by way of apology as much as explanation. "I'm sorry, David."

"You're sorry *what*? Sorry you won't go to bed with me? Sorry you went out to dinner with me? Sorry you invited me up for a drink? Sorry you sat down next to me on the plane? Sorry, but you don't ever want to see me again?"

I tried to absorb his anger without wringing any of it back out of me in his direction. I said nothing. And there was no speech in my silence. I didn't know the answer.

"Anne, that's too many sorries at once. At least, see me again."

"I don't know," I said. "I don't know if I can."

"I'll be back in three weeks," he said. "I won't try to see you again this time, although I'll be here until Monday night." I could see that he was striving for utter reasonableness. "You'll have three weeks to think it over—to think *us* over. Have dinner with me then. You yourself said that dinner isn't necessarily—"

"Ask me then," I said, as if saying something definite. "Ask me in three weeks."

It was a long time—plenty of time.

"I'll call you from Chicago," he said.

"No. In three weeks, when you get back here, I'll tell you. I think both of us could use the time."

"I don't need any three weeks—"

"Take them anyway. Please." It came out firmer than anything else I'd said in the past half-hour.

"All right," he said. "I'll call you from the airport as soon as I get in. Three weeks!"

It suddenly sounded like tomorrow.

He didn't attempt to kiss me. "While you're thinking, don't forget to think about—" He must have read the look on my face fluently, because he stopped short, and nodded. "You'll know what to think about," he said, and left.

Leaving me feeling unfair to him, knowing that I would decide, whatever I decided, only when the three weeks were up. It was the only way I would dare to decide at all. I stood, leaning against the door, for a long while, bemoaning the fact that sheiks on white horses who grabbed you on the gallop, making all decisions superfluous, were extinct. At least in my neighborhood.

I called Munch on Sunday, as I had promised, but I pleaded exhaustion and told her I would rather leave our chat for the following morning.

. . .

It came, as Monday mornings often do, unexpectedly soon.

Munch admired what I had bought at auction, especially the intricately worked coffee service. "How did you know?" she asked.

"Sheer genius. Know what?"

"Mr. Shapley. He was in. He's *looking* for a coffee service. A special one, naturally. He wondered if we were expecting anything in that might be his sort of thing."

"He'll love this!" I was pleased. "And he'll pay a good price for it, too. I told you this trip would be worthwhile."

"It really was?"

I pretended not to understand what she was getting at. I needed more time. "What more proof do you need? It'll take him, I'd say, three weeks to buy it. Then he'll meet our price and be grateful."

Munch tapped her foot. "Hey, lady, *I* am not all business. Your dinner date? The cream silk? Remember?"

"It was very nice."

"What's he like?"

"He's very nice."

"Okay, okay! Should I call Mr. Shapley and tell him about the coffee service?"

"No. Let's just put it in the window. He passes by nearly every day."

"You're bad," said Munch. "Bad."

I moved the pieces over to the window, intending to redo the display at once. I thought over Munch's verdict. "Thanks," I said. "I need all the encouragement I can get."

Returning home from my exercise class Tuesday evening, I encountered Charles Robinson sitting on our stoop.

I stopped directly in front of him. "Yes, it is," I said.

He looked up at me, returning from somewhere. "Sorry?"

"Yes, it is a beautiful evening."

"You're right. Join me on the veranda?" He tapped the stoop beside him.

"You tempt me, but if I do, I'm sure to be sore all over in the morning."

"It's not that hard," he said. "A bit undignified perhaps."

"It's not the stoop," I said, "it's my exercise class." I swung my leotard bag in his direction. "I take class every Tuesday and Thursday evening. Then I take a long hot bath. That's the winning combination."

"Ah, I see. You'd better go on up then." He got up. "You've given me an idea. A bit of exercise wouldn't hurt. Enjoy your tub. Good night."

"Wait!"

He waited.

"I never had a chance to thank you. The Buxtehude. It's extraordinary, your giving it to me."

"You knew it, then? Good."

"I have loved it for years. It's a long story . . . well,

not so long, but I'll save it for another time. Anyway, I had a copy and it got broken. I couldn't find another . . . not the original single. So . . . thank you."

He looked about to say something, but then he just nodded, smiled, and went off on his walk.

I went up the stairs. At the top, I turned and watched him walking toward Central Park. He walked briskly, his head down. He was taking no notice of the evening, he was taking exercise. I regretted for a moment my unwillingness to suffer a little soreness the next day. I could have sat with him, or even offered to join him on his walk. But, maybe, he was only being polite. I was making too much of it, anyway.

Several days later I decided my bathing suit needed replacing. There wasn't much left on the racks. In the limited selection remaining, I found a brown maillot—exactly what I'd had in mind. I felt lucky.

I was inspecting my reflection in the three-way mirror in the dressing room when the salesgirl who had directed me to it opened the curtain and eyed me appraisingly. She nodded, halting her gum-chewing to emphasize the seriousness of the moment. "You really ought to try a bikini," she said.

I welcomed neither her presence nor her advice. I frowned and looked at myself in the mirror again. I saw what she meant. There wasn't a bulge at the thighs or across the back of the suit or near the armpits. For a woman my age, I have a good figure.

Scratch that. I have a good figure.

I glanced at the salesgirl: she had sallow skin and wore an unflattering yellow blouse with a bow she didn't know how to tie.

"If there's a two-piece suit out there in a solid color, I'll try that."

"There's a lavender-and-green print. A small print. Really very conservative," she said.

Now, if you can only learn to wear the right make-up and tie a bow, I bet you'll go far. "I'll try it," I said.

That evening, halfway through my vacuuming, I turned off the Electrolux and changed into the lavender-and-green bathing suit. I opened the door with the mirror on the inside and went back to my vacuuming, stopping every so often to check myself out from every available angle. No disastrous shots; I looked okay. Better than that.

The phone rang, and I shut off the vacuum cleaner, ran into the bathroom, and got the phone on the fourth ring.

"Hello!" I was out of breath.

"Catch you in the shower?" Alex had a way of saying something like that conversationally, without a twinge of potential apology lurking in her voice.

I couldn't help it. I began to laugh. "No, Alex, I was vacuuming."

"What's so hilarious about that?"

"It's hard to explain. It doesn't matter."

"Mother!"

"Daughter!" Again I couldn't help myself. I was suddenly in a terrific mood.

Silence.

Alex was deciding, I knew, whether to ignore me out loud or ignore me period. I put thirty-five cents on ignore me period. Good humor without good and sufficient—and apparent—reason always threw Alex.

"Look, I just called to ask if you can come to dinner Monday night." Thirty-five cents richer—I smiled.

"What are you having?" I said, thinking of Ed Flight and Chicken Kiev.

"I don't know. What's the difference? Are you on a diet or something? You're not having stomach problems?"

Instantly contrite, I said, "No, of course not. And I'd be delighted. What time?"

"Come straight from the shop."

"As is?" I asked, making absolutely sure.

"Sure, why not?"

"You're right." I slipped my arms out of the robe I had grabbed off the hook in the bathroom, letting it fall to the floor. I promenaded in my bathing suit as far as the phone cord would permit. "Why not?"

"Mother, you're sure you're all right?"

"Yes, Alex, I am all right. Good night. See you Monday."

I hung up the phone, picked the robe up off the floor and returned it to its hook. Then I finished my vacuuming, wishing a special delivery letter would arrive or a small fire would break out in the building—in which no one would be hurt, of course.

My terrific mood turned into a restless high by Sunday, a gorgeous, mandatory outdoors, not-too-hot day.

Clad in a denim skirt and a tank top I hadn't worn

in several years, I was walking in the park, indiscriminately enjoying the trees, the old people, the lovers, the squabblers, the kids playing. I recalled that only last week a twenty-two-year-old girl had been raped in this very part of the park. I shivered, and shook my head vehemently to shake off the fear that had welled up in me.

Distracted, I failed to notice Charles Robinson and a companion walking directly in front of me until I was practically on top of them. They must have stepped out of a side path a moment or two earlier, and were deep in conversation. The young man was blond—pale, pale blond—a shade called "champagne" in the romantic English of beauty parlors.

I pulled up abruptly. At my pace I'd catch up with them and pass them by in half a dozen steps. I glanced around for an adjacent path; there wasn't one.

I took off sideways across the grass in the direction of the lake.

Later, sitting on a bench, watching young couples in rowboats, I remembered when Hal and I had taken out a rowboat, on another lake in another season. When we got out in the middle of that lake, he had suddenly begun to shake and confessed that he couldn't swim and was terrified because shore seemed infinitely far away. I had reassured him *somehow*, and he had rowed us back to shore, his pride relatively intact. I had decided, without a moment's hesitation, not to reveal to him that I didn't know how to swim, either. We were married a year before I had to tell him that, and a good half-hour longer before he forgave me.

Making up! How good we'd been at squeezing every drop of pleasure out of that.

Gone.

So was my high.

Hours later, when the phone rang, I was desultorily doing the *Times* crossword puzzle, getting nowhere, and caring not at all.

"Hello," I said.

"Mrs. Durham?"

"Yes?"

"This is Ed Flight. I wonder if you remember me. We met at your daughter's . . ."

Remember Pearl Harbor. Remember the Alamo.

"Yes, Ed, I remember you."

"Good, good. I thought you might have forgotten. How are you?"

"Fine, thank you," I said automatically. Then, thinking fast, I switched off automatic. "As well as can be expected."

"You've been ill?"

I don't know where I got it from, but I had it. "It's nothing . . . imminent."

I listened. The pause was just pregnant enough. A woman can't be a little pregnant but a pause can be. I'd hit it right.

"Oh?" He obviously didn't know how to proceed. That's all right, Ed, come on in, I'm guiding you.

"I'm very sorry," he said.

"Actually, Ed, if I'd met you sooner, it might be . . . nothing."

"Oh!"

"I have stopped smoking, thanks to you, but I guess

it was a *spot* too late," I said slowly. "If you get my meaning."

Silence. He got my meaning.

"Anyway, frankly," I said brightly, "I'd rather not talk about it. Tell me, what was it you called me about, Ed."

"Nothing, nothing really. I just called . . . to say hello."

"Well, wasn't that nice of you. I don't get out as much as . . . and a call from an old . . . friend"—I nearly choked on my cigarette—"well, it helps. It really does."

"It was the least I could do," he said, having apparently already blocked out why he *had* called. "Goodbye, Anne, good luck." He hung up.

"You bitch!" I said out loud as I, too, hung up. Never mind. When vengeance is irresistible, relax and enjoy it. I began to giggle—God forgive me.

Until a sound from next door cut into my self-indulgent laughter as neatly as a sharp, wet knife cuts through birthday cake. Instantly, my little party at Ed Flight's expense was over.

Only one voice carried through the thick old walls, and there were intermittent silences, during which a quieter voice presumably was speaking. I had no idea how long it had been going on, while I was disposing of Ed, but the bitchiness I heard now made me suddenly ashamed of my own.

I heard the door of Charles Robinson's apartment flung open, and a voice in the hallway outside shouted, "You really thought I came here just for *fun!*" And then laughter—ugly, high-pitched and cruel—continuing as someone took the stairs two at a time.

The front door slammed. Mr. Robinson's door closed quietly.

I spent the next two hours fiercely combating the crossword puzzle, until I got every goddamn word. Yet all the words, fitted neatly together, did not blot out my sense that I had something in common with the young man of the blond, blond hair and the bloody language. Something nasty.

In the morning, after a miserable night, I drank four cups of coffee and finished half a pack of cigarettes. I decided I owed Ed Flight an apology. I would get his number from Alex and call him. He was probably in the book, anyway.

No, calling him would be too hard.

And too easy?

It came into my head again: that statement in that article in the *Times*, months ago. I couldn't remember why I'd read the damned article; I'd stopped reading those pieces a couple of years back. I knew it all. I knew I should stop, and I had tried a couple of times. But after twenty-four years, what was the point, anyway? The damage was done.

But the article said that if you stop smoking before you've got lung cancer, no matter how long you've smoked or how much, in eighteen months your lungs are clear. It's as though you'd never smoked. Free and clear.

How that article had made me mad. It couldn't be true. They'd say anything to get people to stop. It couldn't be true.

But if it were . . .

Damn Ed Flight. Damn the *Times*. Why didn't people mind their own business.

I went into the kitchen and removed the two packs of cigarettes left in the carton I had. I took the packs into the bathroom, opened both of them, removed all the cigarettes, and one by one, tore every one of them apart, throwing the contents into the toilet bowl. Periodically, I flushed the toilet so I wouldn't clog it.

It couldn't have taken me more than ten minutes.

12

IT WAS A LONG WEEK, during which I gave David little thought, Charles Robinson no thought, and could not get Ed Flight out of my mind for more than a few hours at a time. I regretted having met him; I regretted having been malicious to him when he called me; most of all, I regretted that I was unable to absolve myself for that without doing such medievally extravagant penance.

I do not mean that I regretted these things and passed on to something else in my life. I mean I spent my days freighted with regret.

And there was time enough for all my regretting, because my days that week held at least forty-eight hours apiece.

The non-smoking days.

The days I virtually did nothing but *not smoke*.

The first full day I didn't smoke, I ate half a pound of cashew nuts, drank a chocolate malted for the first time in a quarter-century, chewed seven packs of gum, and finished off the evening by eating an entire loaf of brown bread blanketed in sweet butter and apricot jam.

I was slightly sick the next morning, and very disgusted. It wouldn't do. It just wouldn't do.

I resolved to take my oral abstinence straight up.

That day I managed to eat normally until late in the evening, unless you count nibbling at thumbnails. I hadn't bitten my nails since I was eight; it came back to me.

At half past ten that night, staring at my eight remaining nails, I decided that I would *do* something.

I baked a double batch of brownies, from scratch of course. Unfortunately, I happen to know a recipe for sensational brownies—brownies so good that they, like *Gulliver's Travels*, should really not be wasted on an undiscerning child.

This grown-up lady downed the lot. It took nearly two hours and a quart and a half of milk, but I did it.

I didn't sleep very well that night.

I didn't feel very well the next morning.

Except for one thing: what I'd always thought of as my early-morning getting-the-night's-frog-out cough seemed to have gone. I would probably have felt a whole lot happier about that if my stomach had felt and looked less like an infant's squishy toy.

That day I ate nothing out of order. I did raise my voice twice at Munch for no good reason.

So the week went, excruciatingly slowly and hurting all the way.

That weekend I spent entirely indoors, despite two sunny, not-too-hot days. I was spring cleaning. It may have been a crazy thing to do, spring cleaning, on an exceptionally nice late July weekend, but it was not entirely irrational. It kept my hands occupied. On Monday morning it was raining heavily. Entirely suitable weather for the way I felt.

Coming out of the house, burdened by two bags of newspapers I had used for some repotting, I couldn't get my umbrella open. I spotted Charles Robinson depositing garbage in one of the cans and hurried down the steps, getting well-dampened in the process.

"Hold it! Please!" I called out to him.

Turning at my voice, he raised his open umbrella so he could see me, held the can lid for me, and made room for me under the umbrella. I deposited my trash. He replaced the lid but continued to hold his umbrella over my head, which prevented me from opening my own. Also, we were standing too close under the one umbrella to talk, somehow.

I smiled, moved out from under his umbrella, and opened mine. "Thanks," I said. "I probably should have made two trips, but I did a major housecleaning this weekend and made enough trips up and down for a month. Then last night I did some repotting and— Do you know any *neat* indoor gardeners?"

"Not any who love their plants enough to transplant them as quickly and painlessly as possible."

"Thanks."

"You're welcome." He started to go back upstairs. "Hope it clears. 'Bye."

"Wait!"

He stopped, and waited.

"Mr. Robinson, would you happen to be free for dinner? Any night this week, I mean. Except Tuesday or Thursday. I have class those nights."

"Your exercise class," he said, smiling.

"Right. Are you?"

"I really don't—yes, of course I'm free. That would be very nice. Especially if it means you'll start calling me Charles."

"It's a deal." I was getting wet despite my umbrella. "Which night?"

"Whatever's best for you."

"How about Wednesday?"

"Wednesday's fine."

"For me too. Seven-thirty all right?"

"Fine. What sort of wine should I bring?"

That stopped me. I had only thought of inviting him five seconds before I did it. A menu was beyond me just then. "Red. Dry," I said, because I like a dry red with almost anything. Gesturing toward the rain, which was gustily having at us, I said, "See you Wednesday if not before. Half past seven."

I dashed then.

I had a feeling that he continued to stand where he was, but I didn't look back.

On Tuesday, during an afternoon lull in the shop, I went out and did my marketing for Wednesday's dinner. It took me longer than I'd anticipated, so when I got back to the shop I apologized to Munch.

"Sorry I took so long. Everything looked so good at Baldini's, I couldn't make up my mind. Ended up with gorgeous zucchini and endive and mushrooms— that big—for salad." I kissed my clustered fingers, Italian fashion.

97

"Who'd you say was coming to dinner?" Munch grinned.

I hadn't. "I don't think I did, did I?"

Munch, undaunted, forged on. "Your mysterious date of a couple weeks back?"

"No."

"You never really said it, in so many words, but I got the feeling you liked him—really liked him."

I glanced down, then away from, my stubby thumbnails. I wanted a cigarette. Whenever I'm disinclined to match Munch's openness, I feel uncomfortable. Just then my discomfort doubled because she had inadvertently pointed out that most of the three weeks was gone, and I had decided nothing.

The hell I hadn't! I'd decided not to smoke. I was obviously wholly capable of making major decisions. Now that I was doing something to prolong my life, the question seemed italicized, one affirmative act suggests another.

Only: to see David or not to see David, which was the affirmative act?

"I've been wrong before," said Munch, still there. Poor Munch. She wasn't being nosy. She cared.

"I liked him," I said. "You were right."

"But he's not the one coming to dinner, the one all the fuss is for?"

"What fuss?"

"Endive is fuss," she said decisively. "A dollar thirty-nine a pound is fuss."

I laughed; I saw her point. "No, he's not the one. I'd tell you." I wasn't really making a fuss. It was just that I seldom have anyone to dinner. And I happen to like endive very much. Munch was looking disappointed.

Best to say it now. "I don't know if I'll be having him to dinner. It's not necessarily an ongoing thing. I mean, I don't know yet, but don't you go counting on it. Okay?"

"Sure, sure," said Munch, the second sure eradicating the first one nicely.

She was bending so far over backward that she was bound to fall in that direction at any moment. "It's Charles Robinson who's coming to dinner."

"Oh," said Munch. An "oh" like that is worth a dozen expressions of disappointment.

"I haven't had an excuse to prepare a proper dinner in weeks." Damn! I hated feeling defensive, and the bloody endive had cost a dollar *fifty*-nine a pound at Baldini's.

"He doesn't sound like much of a reason to me," said Munch, fueling my defensiveness.

"I think he's lonely." I said it without thinking. I should have said, Munch, shut up for a bit.

But I didn't. And she didn't.

"Since when are you an expert on Charles Robinson's emotional temperature? Let alone responsible for regulating it?"

Quick shots of the two young men I'd recently seen with Charles ran on my mind's projector. To me, they bespoke loneliness, but it could be that to him they meant exactly the opposite. I was far from an expert on his emotions. In point of fact, I barely knew the man.

"I'm not," I said. I had to give her that much.

"But I still think he's lonely," I added. I just did.

"So cook him dinner." Munch shrugged, giving up on me, as she has a thousand times in the past. But never for very long.

That evening, after my post-exercise-class bath, I made a spinach soup. It took a while. It always took a little longer than I remembered, but it was worth it.

Before I left for work in the morning, I set the table, fluffed the pillows, and apologized to the plants for giving them slightly short shrift.

Munch didn't mention my dinner the entire day, nor did I. I thought about what she had said, though, and what was behind it. She thought I was butting in where I had little reason to know it would be useful, let alone appreciated.

For God's sake, it was just dinner! The spinach soup would be delicious, the veal would be tender, and I would enjoy the meal *myself*.

And I wasn't lonely.

Since when was terminal loneliness a prerequisite for an appetite? I suddenly felt both pleased and confident about the evening ahead.

By day's end, however, indecision returned.

By the time I got home, it prevailed.

I prepared the salad dressing, showered, made up, and dressed in a pretty pair of mauve lounging pajamas. Then I took one look at myself in the full-length mirror and decided Mr. Robinson—Charles—might get the wrong idea.

That idea, frankly, dismayed me.

Hurrying now, I changed into conservative pants and a silk shirt, checked myself out in the mirror, and got mad. I looked exactly like a woman who is about to entertain a homosexual at dinner and who wants to make absolutely certain he doesn't get the wrong idea. Hell, lady, I told my reflection, if you don't have the wrong idea, he won't get it. Looking nice isn't suggestive, it's plain polite. Besides, it feels nice.

And I didn't, in my navy pants and shirt.

The doorbell rang as I was fastening the hook at the back of the mauve pajamas. I gave the telltale mirror one last chance. No, I did not look like a hetaera, I looked like a rather good-looking woman expecting a guest to dinner. I ran my fingers through my hair and went to the door.

"Hello, come on in," I said, holding the door wide.

Enter Charles. Clean-shaven, smelling of bay rum, wearing a lightweight blazer, a scarf inside his open shirt. *He* had dressed up.

My navy pants and shirt would have been ostentatiously everyday.

"I knew it," he said, smiling at me.

Well done, you, I told myself.

"You did?" I said, not averse to having his implied compliment made explicit. I mean, I *had* changed twice.

"I was sure," he said. "Such good colors, nothing insistent except comfort. It's lovely."

He was talking about my apartment! I couldn't help it, I began to laugh. So much for you, you vamp.

He looked at me quizzically. I stopped laughing. How could I explain? "It's nothing," I said, "a private joke. Of course, you've never been here before," I rushed on, trying to cover my cloddish tracks. "I'd forgotten. Isn't that New York for you? Here we've been neighbors for—what?—two years, and it wasn't until recently that I was in your apartment for the first time."

"It's not quite a month," he said gently, while I weighed the relative merits of pills and a razor. But he rescued me. "What happy-looking plants," he said. "You are a gardener."

"Thank you," I said. Thank you. Suicide would be an exaggerated reaction; it was clear that he was fine.

And I would be, too. I would think before I spoke. It couldn't be that hard. Lots of people do it regularly.

"Now," I said, "do please make yourself at home. What can I get you to drink?"

Again he looked around, this time taking in my small portable bar cart. "May I?" he asked.

"Of course. I'll have a little Scotch and a lot of water. The ice cubes are in the bucket. I'll have lots in mine, please. Now I'll just check on our soup. Back in a moment."

I served coffee on the table in front of the sofa. "Black, the way you take tea?" I asked.

"Yes, please. What an exquisite coffee service."

"It is lovely, isn't it? My husband bought it for me on our tenth wedding anniversary. I had always wanted one. All those nineteen-forties high comedies. You know, I fully intended to be Katharine Hepburn in *Philadelphia Story* when I grew up. Organza dresses and heavy silver. My! I don't think Hal knew what a reckless gift this really was."

"Not so reckless, really. I mean, your shop—you must know a great deal about old silver."

"Some, yes. Of course, when I got this, I never dreamed I'd end up with a silver shop. My fantasies had nothing to do with a career."

He laughed. "But now that you do have the shop, tell me, when you come across a particularly special object or set, how do you bring yourself to part with it? I mean, if you really find such satisfaction . . ."

"It's not the problem you would think. If a customer has that certain appreciative gleam in his eye, you know he's seeing what there is to see, and if he's got the price . . ."

"You wipe away a figurative tear and wrap it up?"

"That's about it. Besides," I went on, a new thought occurring to me, "while I do continue to enjoy the silver I already own, my onetime lust has dissipated. I guess it's because everything—silver, children, plants, friends—everything requires care."

"And the silver doesn't grow?"

"Exactly. It's exquisite, but it isn't alive. And as I get older, I suppose I'm less willing to squander the care I have in me on something . . . finished."

"You should have been a teacher," he said.

"That's why you're a teacher?"

"Of course. There isn't another reason in the world cogent enough to keep me from spending all my days fitting in one more piece in the puzzle of how Elizabeth the First managed to keep the rising tide of parliamentary power at bay—just. When she died, her Scots successor found himself a monarch high and dry, without any power at all."

"Please," I said, "go on."

"That's it. That's the question all my own work has centered on."

"Well," I asked, "what's the answer?"

He laughed. "I'm not sure yet. I've only been working on it for fifteen years, after all."

I didn't press him, but he had intrigued me and I wanted him to say more.

"All right," he said, apparently reading my face. "What I think is—it was sort of a mutual winking. The House of Commons had gained the prerogative of power and they knew she knew it and she knew they knew she knew it, and yet they winked at her and let her hold the reins—and she, consummate politician that she was, had the grace to give them a royal wink back, admitting that she held them—subject to *their* grace."

"She was that good a loser? I'm surprised."

"She was that good a winner. It was the throne which was losing; so long as she occupied it, they would bow before her. She understood it all, you see. Not only that she was the last of her line, and what that meant, but that she was the last of her kind," he said.

"You make her sound like one of a kind," I said.

He smiled. "You should have been a student," he said.

"I have to admit that I didn't think he'd make a decision today," Munch said.

"I told you." I wasn't self-satisfied; I had simply become adept at gauging when a steady customer like Mr. Shapley would cave in and buy.

"But it was nearly five hundred dollars over his price."

"And worth every penny." I emerged from the window, in which I'd been arranging the replacement display for the coffee service I'd bought at auction in Chicago.

"It's three o'clock," Munch said.

I looked at her.

"The day's more than half over and you haven't said a word about your dinner party last night."

"You hadn't asked. And the day nearly half over," I said, succeeding in not smiling.

"That's will power for you," Munch said dryly.

"It was a very nice evening, actually," I said. "My spinach soup was superb."

"And?"

"And the veal was very tender."

"More tender than Charles Robinson, I trust."

"Munch, you're a bigot!" Munch's one-track mind, so far as Charles was concerned, really annoyed me.

"What are you—an *aficionado*?" Munch's pronunciation was impeccable.

I didn't want to laugh.

I tried not to.

You win some, you lose some.

When I got home from exercise class that evening, I found a low box covered with florist's crisp green paper in front of my door.

I sat on the sofa, the box on the coffee table in front of me, for at least three minutes, trying to guess what was under the paper. Then I ripped it open.

In the box were five small plants, not one of which I already had. What an eye that man had! He had not appeared to look over my plants in any detail, yet he had obviously taken some pains to catalog my collection mentally. I was touched.

Just then I heard footsteps coming up the stairs. On the chance that it was he, I went to my door. As I opened it, Charles reached the top step.

"I was hoping that was you I heard. The plants . . .
I just got home— What a marvelous . . ."

He wasn't alone.

Coming up the stairs just behind him was Young
Man #3. The young man smiled at me in a friendly
enough way. Charles simply stared at me, completely
flustered.

"I heard steps on the stairs . . . I just wanted to say
. . . thank you." I closed my door.

Leaning against the shut door, I felt my cheeks
burning. Why in hell had I opened that door? Talk
about butting into his personal life by inviting him
to dinner, now he'll think I'm watching his comings
and goings.

I was still fuming when the phone rang. I let it
ring.

I sat down on the sofa and watched it until it
stopped. Then I leaned back, shut my eyes, and ran
down the list of some of the worse *faux pas* I'd made
in my life. There were a few.

The phone rang again. This time I picked it up on
the fourth ring.

"Hello." My voice sounded perhaps a trifle lower-
keyed than usual, but otherwise unstigmatized by my
latest social atrocity.

"Anne? I was afraid you were still out. I've been
trying to get you for nearly two hours."

No point in pretending I didn't recognize his voice.
"Hello, David. I just got in a few minutes ago." More
or less. "I take an exercise class after work Thursdays.
Tuesdays too." Stop. Take a breath. "When did you
get in?"

"Two hours ago. I just told you that. Two whole hours. I called from Kennedy. When you didn't answer, I took a cab to my hotel. I've been trying you every fifteen minutes since."

"You're here early." Aren't you? Well, I'm not ready. I am not ready.

"I know." He sounded gleeful, like a kid with an unexpected day off from school. "I had a chance to come to look over some figures. They would have kept, but I couldn't. You don't mind? Say you don't mind?"

I mind.

"Anne?"

"I'm here."

"And I'm *here*—and that's ridiculous. Look, you haven't eaten dinner yet, have you?"

"No, but I'm tired, and I need a long bath. To tell you the truth, I'm not very hungry." To tell you part of the truth.

"A drink, then."

"David, first of all, I really do have to take a bath. Otherwise I'll be stiff as a board in the morning." God, I use that excuse a lot. "Besides, I don't feel up to company this evening."

There was a moment's silence. Then, "I didn't mean a drink there."

He'd misunderstood. Or had he? What, exactly, did I mean?

"David, I mean I'm not up to *being* company tonight."

"Anne, please, one drink. In a well-lighted place. You go ahead and take your bath. I'll pick you up in an hour. We'll go someplace nearby . . . one drink."

He certainly didn't sound as confident as he had at the beginning of the conversation. He sounded . . . open. Which was more than I was being.

"David, look, you've caught me by surprise. And I really am tired this evening."

"Anne, listen. I didn't call to tell you I was coming in earlier because you told me not to call you from Chicago. I'm sorry if my coming early has caught you off balance. But surely you've had time . . . and that's all I'm asking for now—a little time. One drink. If you're tired tonight, or caught off guard, all right, don't make it tonight. I'll be here until Monday evening. One drink is all I ask—but that much I do ask. Whatever you've decided, you can tell me then."

"You make it sound so reasonable—and me sound unreasonable to my own ears. All right, I'll come have a drink. In an hour," I said.

"I'll be there. Don't hurry your bath," he said.

I didn't. I sat in the tub for twenty minutes. Wanting a cigarette every one of them.

"Are you asleep?"

"No," I said.

"Then why are your eyes shut?"

"I'm in pain."

Instantly, I felt him shift to get a closer look at my face. I opened one eye and then the other, and spoke as though it were slow work. "I'm starving," I said.

"That's not funny!"

I sat up and threw my legs over the side of the bed.

"No, it certainly is not," I said.

"Where are you going?"

"To get something to assuage my pain."

Then I moved.

But he was faster.

He caught me before I reached the door. He swung me around, glared down at my laughing face, and then kissed my mouth so hard it hurt.

"Don't play games with me," he said.

I put my hand against my mouth.

He removed my hand with his and then kissed me again, very gently. "That better?"

I nodded. He let me go and I started out of the room.

"Anne!" I turned. "Get enough for two."

I got cheese, and bread, and pears, and wine, and knives and napkins and glasses, and we had a picnic in bed. We got crumbs on the sheets and spilled some wine. My mother and my daughter would have disapproved, but I had a fine time.

David ate quietly, seriously. I liked that. Then he looked at me seriously, which I didn't much like.

"Didn't anyone ever teach you it's rude to stare at someone who's eating a ripe pear naked?"

"You still want to be funny," he said.

"What do you want to be?" I asked, knowing perfectly well it was risky.

"Serious," he said. "There are so many things I want to tell you."

I shook my head.

"One thing?" he persisted.

"One *drink*," I said. "And look at us."

And it had only taken one drink. He had gotten his way with me, and it had not been because I'd had more than one drink.

Or taken time to think.

Sober, and mindlessly. That was how I'd brought him home and taken him to bed.

I had wanted him.

My viscera had not misled me in that respect: the bedding part was very, very good.

It was talk I didn't want. Least of all, serious talk.

"I have one question," he said. "And I mean to ask it."

He did, too. I nodded. Might as well get it over with. I didn't have to answer, I only had to listen to the question.

"Are you free for breakfast?" he asked.

I began to laugh, and it was a minute before I realized that he was not laughing. He wasn't even smiling. He was serious. It was a serious question. I stopped laughing.

"I can't," I said. "I mean, not breakfast for two. Tomorrow's a workday for me. Isn't it for you?"

"Sure," he said. "Couldn't you play hooky?"

"Can you?"

"I would."

I have to admit I was surprised. I mean, it didn't seem a serious thing to do. For a man who was so serious about everything.

"Oh," I said, stalling. "Well, yes, ordinarily, I suppose I could. But Munch—she's my partner—her wedding anniversary is Saturday and her husband is taking her away for a long weekend. I couldn't dream of—"

"Of course not," he said promptly. "I guess that leaves out lunches, too. You will have dinner with me?"

"Again?" I said, gesturing at the remains of our picnic supper.

"Can you be serious for two consecutive seconds?"

"What are you feeling so serious *about?*" I was beginning to find David's insistent seriousness out of place. A midnight picnic in bed simply isn't a serious *context*. It's frivolous, and I wanted to feel frivolous about it. About David. About the whole thing. I had to, somehow.

"I'm feeling serious about dinner tonight, dinner Saturday, and breakfast, lunch and dinner Sunday—for starters."

A heavy menu of togetherness—but not all that serious a proposition. So what was I feeling nervous about? What was I afraid of?

I thought of Rita. I hadn't, for years. Rita who had an I.Q. of 158, terrible teeth and the figure of a movie starlet. Once, when we were sophomores in college, she told me that she always went to bed with every guy on the first date; that way, she didn't feel pressured.

What was I feeling pressured about? Here I was, finishing a picnic in bed with an attractive man who liked me, whom I liked—whom I liked in bed very much indeed. So what was I feeling pressured about? Would I like it better if he had offered me some evidence that he was taking me lightly?

Jesus.

"I'd love to have dinner with you tonight—and tomorrow night. And Sunday, I bequeath to you in its entirety."

"That's my girl," he said.

I wouldn't go that far.

I didn't say it. "Listen," I said instead, "what do we do between meals on Sunday? Any ideas?" I had one or two.

"Go to the Cloisters, walk around Chinatown, and go for a ride on the Staten Island ferry," he said.

"My God! You've got everything all worked out," I said, not displeased with his itinerary.

"Not quite everything. But I'm working on it." He smiled.

It was one helluva smile he had.

"You should smile more often," I said.

"Okay," he said.

He took the tray and set it on the floor. Then he reached for me.

The smile was gone from his face.

But I felt much better anyway.

It was noon by the time we started out on Sunday. I was locking the door when I thought of it. "Forgot something," I told David, and ran back inside.

"For the ferry," I said a moment later, waving a scarf at him.

Charles was locking his door, studiously not looking our way.

"Good morning," I said.

"Good morning." He glanced briefly in my general direction and then went on downstairs as if he were in a great hurry.

David looked at me, obviously expecting an explanation.

"That was Charles Robinson. He's my neighbor," I said.

"How do you do, Mr. Robinson," David said.

"I'm sorry. I would have introduced you, but it would have been . . . awkward."

"For whom?"

"It's just that . . . well, we just don't introduce our

guests to each other." Just in case it needed saying. "I don't have many guests."

"That never occurred to me," he said.

"Good," I said. I headed downstairs.

"Does he?"

I kept walking.

"Your Mr. Robinson. Does he have many guests?"

I had reached the bottom of the steps, David just behind me. I had to say something. And yet I suddenly knew I had no intention of telling David anything about Charles Robinson.

I turned to him. "David, this is New York. How would I know? It's practically revolutionary that we know each other's names."

I went on outside. The sun was high and bright.

David took my hand. "All right, then," he said. "Come on. I'll show you New York."

We stood on a lookout point outside the Cloisters, a treasure house of pre-Renaissance art. Below us, the Hudson looked as clean as the sea. Across the river, New Jersey looked as if it smelled like a garden. And above us, the blue-sky sky made clear promises for the rest of the day.

It was not something to discuss, but to share. And we did not discuss it, but shared it.

After quite a long time I glanced at my watch. "Should we go on in now?"

"No."

"It's getting on to two."

"We can leave whenever you want to," he said.

"Without going inside?"

"Sure." He grinned at me. "I've never been inside."

"But on the way over you said you've been here many times—"

"Many times. *Here*. Not inside. You can have the top of the Empire State Building. For my money, this is the best view in Manhattan." He laughed. "And it's free."

What could I say? I loved the somber chaste rooms inside the Cloisters, but there was no denying that the view was a spectacularly beautiful tapestry which could match any museum for subtlety and surpass all for liveliness.

Suddenly, the idea of not going in appealed to me. It seemed a liberated thing to do. I took David's arm and hugged it. "There's something very likable about you," I said.

"I thought you'd never notice."

We walked hand in hand through the narrow streets of Chinatown, looking in shop windows on both sides of each winding street, crossing back and forth several times in every block. I stopped in at a market and picked up some Hoisin Sauce and a bunch of bok choy. David tried to pay. I shook my head. Immediately, he backed off. I liked that.

Finally, we decided on a restaurant in which to eat lunch. It was upstairs, not in the least prepossessing from the outside, and we picked it for no particular reason, although we deliberated between it and another place up the street for some minutes.

Inside, it was even less prepossessing than outside. It was not crowded, but that did not put us off because it was nearly four o'clock, an off-hour. Besides, the patrons were Chinese, a good sign. Best of all signs, the place smelled good.

There was an empty table by the window, and we asked if we might take it. The waiter nodded, and seated us. In a minute he was back with menus for us. They were bulky, bound in stiff cardboard, and written both in Chinese and English.

David looked at me. I nodded, guessing the question. "We'll leave it up to you," David said to the waiter.

The waiter didn't look overwhelmed by flattery. "You only two," he said. "You hungry two?" He looked skeptically from David to me.

"We're both very hungry," I said eagerly.

He smiled then; his front teeth were missing. "All right, then. I feed you." He trotted off to the kitchen.

In a few minutes he returned, carrying a big bowl of soup. He frowned, looking down at our hands, mine between both of David's, in the middle of the table.

"You serious about eating?" he asked sternly.

Hastily, we removed our hands. "Oh, yes," I said. "We're serious about it." I didn't dare look at David.

The waiter set down the bowl of soup and filled both our bowls. "Eat while hot!" he commanded.

We did as we were told. The soup was exemplary, a light but definite broth in which floated at least a dozen ingredients, including two I couldn't place.

The four courses which followed were uniformly good, complementing each other nicely. There was shrimp in a black bean sauce, beef in oyster sauce, shredded chicken in a Szechuan sauce and a dish of superbly crisp mixed greens and mushrooms.

Finally, when empty and half-empty dishes filled

the table, I sat back. "I'm not sure I'm ambulatory," I said.

The waiter came over, inspected each dish, then looked from David to me. "Finished?" he asked non-committally.

"I'm afraid so. It was all marvelous," I said. "But our two friends weren't very hungry."

The waiter frowned again. Then, as he got my joke, the frown eased and he flashed a gap-toothed smile at me. "Is all right," he said. "You did all right. You want dessert now?"

"No!" David said.

"No! Please!" I said.

All three of us laughed then.

The waiter picked up the teapot, which he had already refilled once, and shook it. "I bring more tea," he said, and left us.

We were both apparently too full for conversation, but the waiter was back in a minute anyway. He held a full teapot and a plate with two fortune cookies.

He placed the plate on the table between us. "You pick first," he instructed me, and walked off, obviously confident of my obedience.

"He hasn't misled us so far," David said.

I picked up the cookie nearest me, broke it open, and read the fortune on the narrow slip of white paper inside.

David looked at me expectantly, but instead of handing him the slip of paper, I pointed to the remaining cookie.

"Okay," he said. He picked up the cookie, broke it apart, and read the contents of the slip of paper inside. Then, with pointed graciousness, he handed it to me.

I took it and read it. Then, managing a straight face, I handed him mine, which was identically romantic. He read it, looked at me, and we laughed together.

"There must be a special box," I said.

"Why not think it was the gods. Chinese gods are very powerful," David said.

"The Chinese don't believe in gods."

"I bet the ones who've met our waiter do."

I laughed as the waiter came back with the bill, not even the vestige of a smile of self-satisfaction on his face. David picked up the bill, took out money, counted it out carefully and exactly, and handed it to the waiter.

The waiter bowed us out with enormous aplomb.

On the street again, I said, "I can barely walk, but it was worth it. A superb meal."

"And a bargain at that," David said.

I hadn't been able to help noticing; it was the order in which he laid the bills on the table. I saw no reason to let it pass, since it was a nice thing for David to do. "Not after you left him a ten-dollar tip," I said.

"That was no tip, that was an offering to those gods," he said.

"My plane is at nine this evening."

It was the first time David had spoken since he'd said "good morning" after we'd made love to the ringing of the alarm. I had never before truly appreciated the sedate baritone sound of my alarm.

We had both been hurrying since then. A late start. I was not used to sharing my bathroom, and apparently neither was David. Noticing that, I allowed myself a single thought about where he was going on that nine o'clock plane. If he had his own bathroom at home, did that mean he had his own bedroom? No, it would not bear thinking about. Fortunately, there was no time.

"Look," he said, "I couldn't get out of a meeting later today, not once I was here. But I think I can get out by seven. Have a fast bite with me?"

I nodded.

"We still haven't had a proper dinner. I'd write you an IOU but I'd need a ream of paper." I knew he was trying to get me to smile. I wasn't sure why I couldn't seem to. I tried.

I tried again. I think I succeeded that time.

"Where can I reach you? Here?"

"I'll wait in the shop," I said. "There's always something I can do there, and it's closer to downtown."

"I'll call the minute the meeting breaks."

He called at five to eight.

I said I'd grab a cab and pick him up at his hotel; he had to pick up his things. I sounded calm and collected.

It was eight-fifteen when he emerged from the revolving doors and got into the taxi I had waiting.

"Twenty-four West Seventy-fourth Street," he said to the driver. "Then we're going to Kennedy Airport."

"You'll miss your plane if we go to my place first. Driver, go directly to Kennedy. Then I'll be coming back in to the Seventy-fourth Street address."

The taxi driver slowed, his eyes on David in the rear-view mirror. David nodded.

"Okay by me," the cabbie said grudgingly, as though he felt called upon to be tolerant.

He started making his way through the intricacies

of New York traffic as David took my hand. I was reluctant, because I knew it wasn't as cool as I was managing to keep my voice, but David wanted it and he took it.

"I'm so sorry that the meeting lasted longer than I'd anticipated. There was a last-minute hassle—there was just no way I could walk out before it was over."

"Did you win?"

"The side that's for me won," he said precisely.

"Good. Anyway, I understand," I said.

"That makes it worse," he said.

"I didn't say it didn't matter. I said I understood."

"Have I told you yet—"

I squeezed his hand hard to silence him, nodding in the direction of the cabbie. I am convinced that cabbies have something in common with slightly deaf people: they can hear anything through that plastic bulletproof partition they really want to hear.

"All right, not now," David said reluctantly. He sat back, holding tightly to my hand, and we were silent the rest of the drive out to Kennedy.

As we approached the terminal entrance, the taxi slowed and stopped. David turned to me. In the rearview mirror, the cabbie watched us unabashedly.

"I'm not allowed to stand here," he said.

"You have to hurry, anyway," I said to David. "You'll miss your plane!"

"Not much," he said, and even his sideways smile was more sideways than usual. But then he raised my hand to his lips and got quickly out of the cab.

He bent his head back into the window. "I'll be back!" he said urgently.

I smiled, feeling as if I had on a facial mask that was ready to crack. "You'd better! You owe me a dinner!"

David nodded solemnly, then turned and hurried into the terminal.

"West Seventy-fourth Street, right?"

"Right," I said. Forcing myself to admit I could no longer see David, I made myself sit back. I took a deep breath. Call it a sigh.

"It'd be different if you were married," the cabbie said, picking up speed. "I know—just ask me!"

But I didn't.

I couldn't sleep. I got up out of bed, got myself a glass of milk, and sat down on the sofa.

I wanted a *cigarette*.

All the days David had been with me, I had managed to put smoking out of my mind. Now I wanted a cigarette badly. The store on the corner would still be open.

I got up, filled a watering can, and went from plant to plant, feeling the soil of each to see which ones might want watering. Of course none did. Despite David's being there that morning, I had not forgotten to water them, and even a coleus wouldn't want watering until the following morning.

Besides, I was being selfish. Plants don't respond well to watering except in the morning. They have a preferred routine just the way people do. I wouldn't want my three meals rescheduled, with breakfast at ten P.M., lunch at one A.M., and dinner at six in the morning.

Well, no harm done. No need to shower myself with a stiff spray of guilt. I hadn't actually watered a single one. I hadn't used them badly just because I had to do *something* if I wasn't going out for that pack of cigarettes.

There was something I could do.

I could cry.

As if in direct response to the thought, tears welled. Real ones.

Through them, I turned on my plants, working out some vestigial Old Testament guilt toward them in anger, I suppose. You get through the night all on your own, I accused them. It's the mornings you can't get through. Then you want attention. But when I need you to need me—you're damned placid about being self-sufficient.

I plunked down the watering can, and did not wipe up the resulting spillage. The table was well waxed; it would survive.

We all survive.

Damn! I didn't want to miss him. Not a man I wasn't in love with. And I knew I was not in love with David. Despite the smile that I found really captivating, and the sex which was better than good enough, there was that seriousness that made me uneasy. I am not an unserious person, but David was serious in a way that made me think of someone strenuously pumping water from a well . . . that wasn't really very deep.

I didn't love him.

In Chicago, there might be someone who loved him.

Unlike David, I had a sense of the boundlessness of marriage. I grabbed my keys and went out. I walked to the corner store, then on past it and around the block.

Then again, and a third time.

I went home without cigarettes, and with a certain

quiet outrage at Ed Flight and David Meray and all men because of whom you do things for the wrong reasons.

I was wrapping a package for a customer. Tying a white ribbon around the silver-on-grey striped paper, I made a good bow. The package looked nice. I handed it over to the customer.

"Thank you," I said. "I'm sure they'll enjoy it." My voice sounded insincere to my ears. I had taken a dislike to the woman as soon as she had walked into the shop nearly an hour ago. Our contact since then had not ameliorated my first impression.

"At this price—" she started, glanced at my face, and stopped. I can, when the occasion calls for it, assume quite a formidable expression.

After the door clicked behind her, I said "At this price" twice, my imitation exaggerated but not markedly off base.

"She was bad, I admit, but not the worst example of humanity we see in an average week," said Munch. "Did my being out for three days make things hard for you?"

"Your being out for three days made things *fine*."

"Gee, thanks."

"I don't mean that I didn't miss you, because I did. But you know the city practically empties out on warm weekends, so Saturday, which is the only day that might have been hectic, was quiet as a lake. Did you and Lew have a marvelous time?"

"I did. I think four days of lying in the sun and

having breakfast in bed and staying up late is more of the easy life than Lew can stand in one shot. I dread the day he retires."

"Don't worry about it today, okay?"

"It is a bit premature," Munch said. "Like the four grey hairs I found this weekend."

"What were you doing looking for grey hairs?"

"I was looking for *no* grey hairs."

"You're gorgeous. If you turned white by Friday, you'd be gorgeous."

"And eighty."

"Hey, you come back from a four-day holiday looking ravishing and sounding like doom. Did something happen while you were away?"

Munch looked away. "No," she said, very quietly.

Oh. Dear God, I knew what she was referring to. I have no idea how I knew, but I knew.

I had to say something about something else, fast, or Munch would be sorry later. Munch likes to talk about personal things—mostly mine, seldom hers. Not once, in the twenty-two years she and Lew had been married, had Munch so much as hinted at anything that might or might not be happening between them in bed.

So I wasn't supposed to know there was anything wrong.

But I did.

"I had an unexpected visit this weekend," I said. Merry Christmas, dear Munch.

She turned. She was all right—a clean save. "Who from?" she asked.

"Your mysterious stranger." I smiled.

"*Your* mysterious stranger—he's back?"

She looked so pleased I hesitated to say it. "He was here. He left last night."

"For where?"

"Home," I said. It sounded like a place where people wore odd costumes and spoke an undecipherable dialect.

"Sorry," Munch said, her face repeating the word.

"Don't be. It's all right. He just doesn't live here," I said matter-of-factly, whether to cover my own embarrassment or Munch's, I don't know. It didn't cover much.

I looked at Munch. Sometimes, when she's putting two and two together, you can almost see her counting on her fingers emotionally. She so transparently wants the bottom line to come out right.

Now she didn't look sure.

"He's *not* mysterious. You make him sound like Gary Cooper riding into town alone, with too much past and no future. Look, he lives in Chicago, that's all." I sighed. "His name is David Meray," I said, and took a breath because I wasn't sure what to say next. Munch is conventional in certain ways, and besides being my best friend, she's also a married woman. She has that in common with David Meray's wife. But she did want to know about him, and suddenly it seemed easier to tell her than not to. "He comes to New York once a month or so."

"And the rest of the time he lives . . . in Chicago."

"He lives at home," I said. "His home is in Chicago." It was getting easier. I could get used to saying that. Maybe.

Conventional or not, married lady or not, Munch

is my friend. She did her emotional arithmetic, taking her time, then she said, "I see." Really nicely.

That did it.

"You do? I'm not sure I do. I mean, what's the point?"

"Anne, I only now found out his name. But I knew weeks ago that he wasn't just anybody. He's someone special."

"Just for argument, say he is. So?"

"I would say then, old friend, that *that's* the point."

"Once a month, for a couple of days? That's what it would be." That's what it *would* be, and I hated that.

Her face changed then. The sympathy went out of it, replaced by pain. "How much happiness do you think anybody gets?" Her voice was tight and harsh. She looked down at her desk, shuffled a few papers. When she looked up at me again, her face was closed and her tone was conversational. "Besides," she said, "you're not going to stop living the other twenty-eight days each month. The time with him will be on top of the rest of your life, not instead of it."

I stared at Munch.

I saw my friend, who sometimes showed signs of possessing the spiritual open-handedness of a saint.

I saw a woman carapaced in naïveté as only a woman who's never had an affair can be.

I saw a woman who had just spent a four-day anniversary holiday with a husband who had not, I knew, made love to her.

I looked at Munch and I saw how unsimple life is.

Mine no more than anyone's.

13

WHEN I WAS THIRTY-FIVE or thereabouts, I resolved never again to finish a book just because I'd started it. But I never extended that vow to concerts. I had never left one before it was over.

I just could not sit through any more. Out of loyalty to Mozart, I really felt I had no choice. As I reached the exit door a voice just behind me said, "A fellow refugee, I presume?"

It was Charles Robinson. "How anyone could make that horn concerto sound *drab* . . ." My indignation overflowed into silence.

"You sound as though you could use an antidote. Would you like to have a drink?"

"Would I!"

He gestured to the restaurant-bar behind us in the hall, his eyebrows a question mark.

"Perhaps a bit too close to the scene of the crime?" I suggested.

"I have an idea," he said.

"I'm sure it's a good one. Lead the way."

Charles looked pleased; I would almost have said flattered. I couldn't see why. After all, he'd had the sense to walk out on the Mozart debacle. He'd know where to recuperate properly from it.

Outside, he hailed a cab.

He took me to the Bemelman's Bar at the Carlyle. Without doubt, in my opinion, the very nicest drinking place in the city under any circumstances. Today the good jazz piano in the background was exactly the right musical antidote to misplayed Mozart.

When our drinks came, he raised his in a toast. "To Mozart!"

"To Mozart!" I said.

We had two drinks apiece, a pleasant talk mainly about other, better, Mozart concerts we'd heard at other times, in other places.

When we came out of the Carlyle, he asked, "Are you headed home?"

"Yes."

"Me too," he said. "It's such a soft time of day. Would you be interested in walking part of the way?"

He was full of good ideas.

At the bottom of the steps to the house, Charles turned to me, sincerely apologetic. "I'm sorry. Honestly, I didn't mean to make you walk all the way home."

"You didn't make me. I assure you, if I'd wanted to stop walking, I'd have mentioned it. Actually, I used to take walks at dusk frequently. I used to walk home from the shop the first couple of years, but these days it doesn't seem prudent to walk alone at this hour, so I usually don't. You did me a favor, look at it that way."

"What a gift you have for turning something around to show its best side," he said.

We started up the steps together. Halfway up, he stopped. "Look, I know this is awfully short notice, and you probably have other plans . . ."

I shook my head. I planned to wash my hair. I don't count that having plans.

"Well!" He looked at once pleased and taken aback. "Well, good! Do you like Chinese food?"

"Of course."

"Shrimp in hot sauce?"

"You're making my mouth water," I said.

"That's wonderful—I mean, that's what I'm about to make. You see, they looked so fresh this morning, I got carried away and bought much too much for one. So if you've nothing better . . ."

"I'd *like* nothing better," I said.

It was true. And not just because he's . . . safe. Still, my love life is complicated enough, and Charles is interesting and amiable and . . . easy.

"Come right away. We can talk while I prepare the vegetables—or you could come a bit later, if you'd prefer."

"Now is fine."

We reached our floor. "I'll be in in just a minute," I said.

True to my word, I rang his bell in not much more than a minute. When he opened the door, I held up my cleaver for inspection. "Have cleaver! Can chop!"

It turned out we were both good at it. Quick and accurate, and relaxed enough about its use to be able to carry on a conversation at the same time.

I watched him work on the shrimp. I'm a good cook myself, so I appreciated his economical movements and his understated culinary style. And the food smelled sensational.

We sat down, bowls of rice and plates of shrimp in hot pepper sauce before us. I lifted chopsticks beside my place, and shook my head ruefully.

"Is something the matter?" Charles asked. "Did I forget something?"

"Not exactly. But . . . I never learned, I'm afraid."

"I'm sorry?"

"These," I said. "I don't know how to use them."

He was surprised and didn't attempt to hide it, which was all right. It wasn't as if I'd confessed to something I was sensitive about, like a predilection for kleptomania.

"But you know so much about Chinese cooking," he said. "And you're a whiz with that cleaver."

"Thanks. But if you don't give me a fork, I'll starve."

"Of course!" He was up and back in a moment. He held out a fork to me, then pulled it back as I reached for it. "You wouldn't like to learn?" he asked.

I was hungry. The shrimp smelled marvelous. Still, I'd always wanted to learn to use chopsticks. I'd just never gotten around to it. Charles took my silence for an answer and held the fork out to me again.

I took it, looked at it, then I put it down and picked up the chopsticks. "How does this compare in complexity with Elizabethan power politics?" I asked.

He laughed; it was a soft laugh without edges. "Much less complicated, I promise. Look . . ." he said, and showed me how to hold and manipulate the chopsticks, demonstrating until I got it right.

A full five minutes later I succeeded in transferring a shrimp from the bowl to my mouth without dropping it en route. "It's delicious!"

He grinned. "You just worked up an appetite."

"You know," I said, "I've always thought of the Chinese as an exceptionally dexterous people, but it wasn't as hard as I thought it would be to learn."

"Good student . . . good teacher . . . disappearing shrimp," he said.

"Confucius?" I smiled.

"Robinson"—he laughed—"and not at his best. At least, let it be true," he said. "Eat."

I picked up another shrimp with the chopsticks and consummated the procedure rather handily. Then again, and yet again.

In no time I said, "Good student . . . good teacher . . . disappearing shrimp."

Then I began to laugh with the sheer pleasure of having a new skill and a new friend.

14

I LIFTED MY FALSE ARALIA to check it out once again. With patient diligence I had finally cured it of a nasty case of mealybugs. I inspected the stem carefully and found no signs of recurrence. New leaves, growing with the aristocratic grace which validates this plant's Latin name, *Dizygotheca elegantissima*, verified its return to health.

"My, you really are your good-looking self again," I told Elegantissima, which is what I call her, because I wouldn't think of calling her false anything.

The phone rang.

I replaced Elegantissima in her saucer and answered. "Hello?"

"Hello, darling."

"Hello, David! Hello!"

"Free tonight?"

"Only until breakfast."

"Shall we start with that dinner I owe you?"

"Now that's a handsome thought!"

"Half past seven?"

"Half past seven."

"Anne?"

"I'm here," I said.

"God, I wish I were. Make it seven-fifteen?"

"I'll be ready at ten after," I said.

"That's nearly eleven hours away," David said.

"You make it sound like an eternity."

"You make it feel like an eternity."

"David, I'd better go. If I get to work late, I may have to stay late."

"Not true. You're your own boss. And a nicer boss a person couldn't have."

"David, have you been to Ireland in the past three weeks?"

"No, why?"

"You sound as if you've kissed the Blarney stone."

"You really had to say it."

"Don't start!"

"You're the one who started, with all your talk of kissing."

"David!"

"I'm coming over there right now."

"I won't be here."

"You really wouldn't, would you?"

"Don't you have appointments today?"

"Sure. Four of them."

"Then the time will pass quickly. See you at ten past seven."

But the day didn't pass quickly, at least not on my end. We had one customer in the morning who spent an hour and a half, and that was all she spent.

Finally, at midafternoon, I succumbed to a temptation which had been gnawing at me all day. I told Munch I'd be back in half an hour and hurried over to an exclusive little shop two blocks away from ours. Two days earlier I'd seen a smashing black dress in the window. It wasn't in the window any more, but I went in anyway.

Yes, they still had it, and in my size. The saleswoman brought it out.

Proximity did not diminish its glamour. It was devastatingly simple. Even a strand of real pearls would be extraneous.

It was one hundred dollars too expensive.

I tried it on.

"It's you, madame," the saleswoman said.

Even if it wasn't me, it sure did a lot for the me who is.

The excitement of buying such a special dress—at such an outrageous price—speeded up what was left of the afternoon.

We had dinner and each other that night.

Next day we had lunch and skipped dinner. This affair was really marvelous for my figure, if not for my budget.

I told David to get into bed and wait for me, I had a surprise. It was a pale sea-green satin nightdress, bias-cut, clingy and smooth. I had bought it between lunch and bed. Fortunately, it had been another quiet day in the shop.

Now David's face, as I came out of the bathroom, confirmed that I had not been rash to buy the night-dress. He held out his arms to me, and I got in beside him. He leaned back again, holding me in the crook of one arm, the other supporting his head. I glanced up at him, slid out of bed, and got an extra pillow out of the closet. I placed it behind his head, and went around to my side to get in again.

"All the comforts of home," said David, pleasure deep in his throat.

It hit me like a slap, that contented remark. I got into bed, of course. I am not inclined to make scenes and I didn't want David to see how hurt I was. But I couldn't quite make myself slide back into the niche his bent arm made.

I felt him look over at me. "Anne," he said, regret in the softness of his voice. "It's an expression. It's just an expression."

I nodded, continuing to look at the ceiling. It was not a particularly productive ceiling to look at, but it's the only one I had. I wished it had cherubs to count.

David leaned close to me, and with his hand, turned my face toward his. "Anne, don't cut me out when everything is . . . when we're this . . . Anne, I think I love you."

His hand held my chin; I couldn't turn away. And there was no turning away from the seriousness in his eyes. That damn seriousness of his!

But who was being overly serious now? It *was* just an expression. Nothing more. It was something people said. I would not think about it any more.

And then there was no time for it.

Lunch the following day was luxurious and delicious. David was at his most entertaining, describing a meeting he'd had that morning: he was graphic, funny and victorious.

He was a good winner, was David.

Over coffee I said, "Tonight I'm going to show off for you."

"You did a superior job of that last night, it seems to me." He smiled, and I realized what was so captivating about that sideways smile of his. It was like one of those thigh-high slits in an otherwise ascetically cut black gown—its very unexpectedness made it sexy.

"You're a salacious old man," I said, smiling back at him. "I meant my culinary skills. I'm going to make one helluva Chinese chicken dish for you. How does that sound?"

"Beautiful!" he said. "Not as beautiful as you in that green nightgown, but pretty damn beautiful." His enthusiasm was unmistakable. "Only, can it keep?"

"Not long enough," I said, smiling indulgently. "You really *are* like Marlene Dietrich."

"I'm what!"

"Sexy," I said. "Anyway, Chinese food is like a soufflé, it won't keep for sex."

He reached across the table and took my hand. "I meant a couple of weeks, darling," he said.

It took me a moment. He cut into it.

"I'm sorry, darling," he was saying, "but I got a message this morning. There's an urgent board meeting on a major project. It's scheduled for eight A.M. I have to be there in person to see how the ball is going, so I can get in the right position to catch it when the time comes. To make things worse, I have to get back tonight to get filled in—or I'd wait until morning to leave."

I nodded, to signify that I was listening. It was all I could manage.

"You understand?" he asked. "You do understand?"

But I didn't. And it took me yet another moment before I could lay my finger on what it was that bothered me. Then I said, "No, David, I don't. I don't understand how all through lunch you've pretended to be in such a good mood—acting as though nothing was wrong."

"But I haven't been pretending," he said. "Nothing is wrong. Anne, look, I live every moment we have together fully—in its own time frame. Every moment is present tense. We're together now. Now is all that counts. Don't spoil it, Anne. Don't start watching the time we have together. Enjoy it . . . love it, the way I do."

"For tomorrow we die?" The edge in my voice was sharp and it didn't miss him. He flinched.

"Of course not! We're not going to die. We—you and I together, like this—we're going to go on and on and on . . . and I'll be back before you know it."

"I see what you mean," I said, very carefully.

But you're wrong.

"I knew you would," he said, letting go my hand at last.

15

I TOOK AN EXTRA EXERCISE CLASS every week, and that helped. Some. The weeks between visits when David was away passed by the hour for me.

I missed him physically. When I was not having an affair, which was most of the time, my sexuality lowered, like a riverbed in a dry spell. But having sex made me want to have more sex: the more sex I had, the more I wanted.

I also missed David's funny seriousness. Not that I liked it—I didn't, and I had a feeling I'd grow to like it even less eventually. But right now I found myself missing it.

The playfulness David brought out in me, I missed that a lot. It is a knack I have which comes and goes. David brought it out in two ways—partly as contrariness to spotlight his seriousness, but mainly because he made me feel womanly, and that always makes me feel girlish in the remaining good ways.

So I missed David.

And I minded that he didn't seem to miss me. Also, I suspected that his use of the present tense alone indicated a limited emotional vocabulary. His lopsided seriousness and blinkered view of time made me edgy, and when he was away, they grew in my memory bank while his smile, long-distance, was non-negotiable.

Therefore, I didn't look forward unconditionally to his next visit; rather, I felt that the sooner it came, the better.

I marked off the days on my kitchen wall calendar. It had been more than three weeks since David's last visit—that made for a lot of X's. My calendar was beginning to look X-heavy. As I stood and looked at it while the teakettle came to the boil, I was beginning to have a heavy feeling. Crossed-out days. Days that didn't count, except insofar as they drew a path to the days of David's visit.

I couldn't afford a near-month of days that didn't count. Not at my age.

I recoiled at that. *My age?* Since when was that a sore subject with me? In fact, it was a subject I hardly thought about. Certainly, I wasn't twenty. But then, I wouldn't be twenty again for anything.

The kettle whistled. I poured the boiling water into a small pot of strong Irish breakfast tea, and was adding a teaspoon of honey when the phone rang.

I lifted out the honey spoon, covered the teapot, and went to answer the phone.

"Hello?"

"Anne? It's Charles."

"Hi. You sound far away."

"I'm not. Look, I know I should ask in a more roundabout fashion, but are you . . . alone?"

"Yes, I am. Charles, is something wrong?"

"No . . . not exactly." I heard him inhale, getting up courage. "It's this. Could you stand some company? *Mine?*"

Something was wrong. I felt my toweled hair. It was less than an hour since I'd washed it. So what? "Would you like to come over for coffee?"

"Frankly, what I'd really like is to take a walk— but not alone. I know it sounds funny . . ."

My hand went again to my terry-cloth turban. I could get my hair relatively dry in a few minutes with a hand blower. It was a mild evening; going out with slightly damp hair wouldn't do me any harm. "Actually," I improvised, "I was thinking of taking a walk myself, it's such a lovely evening. But I decided I'd better not— you remember, I mentioned to you once how shockingly prudent I've become about walking by myself after daylight goes. Just give me ten minutes. I'll ring your bell."

"Thank you," he said, sounding inordinately grateful, I thought.

"Ten minutes at most!" I said.

We walked quite a ways in total silence. I didn't mind. It was a lovely evening; the stickiness of the day seemed like a faraway discomfort.

Finally, he said, "I just couldn't stand that apartment tonight. I couldn't be alone there . . . not tonight."

I nodded, which was silly, because he was looking dead ahead. Besides, I had no idea what, specifically, he was talking about, although I could certainly remember nights I had found my place unbearable in the months after Hal's death. It was perfectly natural.

Then Charles said, "I couldn't be with a . . . stranger, either." I still didn't know what was bothering him, but I certainly knew that feeling. And I was glad we weren't merely neighborly strangers any more.

I turned slightly toward him, slowing my pace. He stopped. "Today is Raymond's birthday," he said without looking at me. Then he did, and said, "Isn't that silly?" And before I could respond, he had begun to walk again, more quickly than before.

I caught up with him and kept pace. Perhaps two whole minutes went by. I hadn't thought of anything to say, and it seemed too late to say anything. Obviously, it wasn't silly, but that wasn't a *response*.

Then, almost inaudibly, Charles said, "I miss him."

This time I was certain there was nothing I could say, but my hand responded of its own accord and touched his arm. Only for a moment, and he showed no sign of having noticed.

We walked for half an hour longer. I don't think we said more than twenty words between us.

Later, lying in bed, I had a siege of sadness for Charles's loss, and because I had been unable to offer him any real comfort.

16

I WAS TRYING ON A NEW RED-AND-PURPLE CAFTAN I had bought for my dinner-at-home with David, when the phone rang.

"Hello!" I just knew it was he.

"It's me," he said.

"Hello, you! You're early; you're not due till morning. But do not for a moment feel unwelcome. Come on over—"

"Anne, listen. I can only talk a minute."

Oh, for the good old days when you could tell when a phone call was long-distance.

"You're not coming." Calm, the voice I heard. How

ridiculously calm I sounded—why not holler and stomp and cry. Really, it would be more seemly.

He was speaking—low, but he was going on, he was still there on the other end of the line. He wasn't coming here, but he was still there.

"Of course I'm coming," he said. "Just not tomorrow."

"Oh." A reasonable response, recording a fact. "I see." Eminently reasonable, that. Too fucking reasonable.

"God, I hope you do," the voice whispered. "Because, believe me, making this call hasn't been easy."

He didn't mean having to make it; he meant getting to make it.

Tough titty. Dear God, I've never said—or thought—that before in my life.

The voice, that low whispering discreet stranger's voice, went on. We were still connected, so to speak. "Look, I have to get back. I'll call you just as soon as I know when I can make it. Good night, darling."

Disconnect. Gone. Pffft.

Back to wherever he had to get back to. Back to his reasonable, respect-the-bounds marriage.

God, I was angry!

I was still holding the dead receiver. I put it back where it belonged. And sneezed. Twice. Hard.

I had sneezed several times in the shop that day. Munch asked if I was coming down with something, and I assured her there was no chance, not with David coming tomorrow. This last I kept to myself. Munch is very down-to-earth about things like colds: she refuses to believe they can be forestalled by will power, but I know better. I had no intention of getting a cold with David coming tomorrow.

David wasn't coming tomorrow.

I sneezed again.

The obverse of mind over matter is mind going soft when it no longer seems to matter. Nonsense! Just because you now have nothing better to do for the next couple of days is no reason to get a cold.

I walked toward my bedroom, concentrating on not sneezing. I made it to the door. Inside, I removed my new caftan. I was already feeling a critical case of disappointment coming on, and I didn't need a cold to compound that misery.

Half an hour later I sat in an ancient chenille robe listening to the Buxtehude "Aperite," feeling supremely unserene and sipping a hot toddy. Perhaps the old robe, which I never wore except when I had a cold, and the toddy, another accouterment of bodily malaise, would encourage my embryonic cold to arrive full-born.

Might as well get it over with, because I couldn't feel *much* worse.

The phone rang. I looked at it with distrust. It rang again. I remembered how enthusiastically I'd answered it not forty-five minutes ago. Scratched like that, the still-fresh wound began to bleed again. Let the bloody phone ring.

It did—again and again. I picked it up.

"Hello?" I did not sound sick. A little petulant maybe, but not sick. This cold was taking its own good time arriving.

"Hello, it's Charles. I know it's terribly late, but this just came up, and I went to your door and you're playing your phonograph, and I had to get hold of you tonight or it would be too late."

"It's all right, really it's all right. I was just sitting

here thinking about the mental health crisis in this country," I said. "How are you?"

"My mental health is improving, thank you," he said, a chuckle in there somewhere.

"I didn't mean it that way."

"Nonetheless, I am better. Much. Thanks largely to you. But look, I wouldn't call at this hour to express gratitude, I am calling about something that *won't* keep. A friend of mine just sent over to me two tickets to the Horowitz recital—he and his wife have both come down with the flu—and, well, I'd like you to have them. It's tomorrow night. That's why I had to reach you this evening. Can you use them?"

Can you use a Horowitz concert? Can you use a spiritual sauna? "Well, of course I'd like to go. Who wouldn't? I'm not insane—even if I am indulging a prurient interest in mental health at the moment."

"Good. It's settled, then. I'll slip the envelope under your door—"

"There is one problem," I said. "Having just said who wouldn't want to go hear Horowitz, I now realize that I don't know a single person who'd really appreciate the recital properly—except you, of course. So I'm afraid that if you're tied up, one of the tickets will have to go to waste."

"Oh no it won't!" he said. "I'd love to go with you."

"Well," I said, "that's fine. Now, why on earth didn't you suggest that in the first— Never mind, I'd be delighted to go with you."

"That makes two of us. Look, do you like Japanese food?"

"Really, you don't have to—"

"Do you like it?" His voice was firm. He sounded

like a teacher eliciting an important progression of thought from a pupil.

I smiled and said, "Yes, I like Japanese food. I like Indonesian food and Senegalese food and Texan food . . ."

"I'll remember," he said. Then, quickly, "Would six-thirty be too early?"

"Six-thirty would be fine."

"Good. Good night."

"Good night."

"Anne?"

"Yes?"

"Do you know how to make real Texas chili?"

"It's one of my specialties."

"Do you use cumin?"

"Naturally."

"In what proportion to the chili powder?"

"Ah, now that's a question. And the answer happens to be a secret."

"Oh." *Disappointment.*

"But don't give up. I once told somebody. Of course, we'd been friends for twenty years."

"Well, with nineteen years and ten months to go, I guess I'd better get my rest. Good night again."

"See you tomorrow," I said, and wondered why I was smiling so.

I sneezed twice then, and stopped smiling. I took two aspirin, a large glass of orange juice, and went immediately to bed. Sternly, I informed my body that I had changed my mind again. I had something good to do tomorrow and I didn't wish to be hampered by a cold.

No cold no cold no cold no cold. I fell asleep reciting it to myself.

I dreamt I was lying on a beach on an island in the South Pacific. In front of me, standing on a flat parcel of white sand, stood a grand piano. Horowitz sat at the piano. I looked around. There were only two people on the entire expanse of beach, Horowitz and me. He began to play. For me alone.

He never played better.

17

FOR HOROWITZ, I WORE MY NEW BLACK DRESS. Fortunately, for the purpose of sitting Japanese-style, the skirt was full-cut.

I allowed Charles to order, and I used chopsticks in public for the first time. Charles was very pleased with my performance. So was I.

"But I have to admit, I've been practicing."

"Well, it shows," he said. "You know, I didn't always love music. In fact, from the ages of seven to nine I loathed it. That was the period during which my mother underwent her Charles-really-must-learn-to-play-the-piano phase."

"Why did you have to learn to play the piano?"

"Because we had one."

"Did she play, your mother?"

"No."

"Did your father play?"

"No."

"Your sisters . . . brothers? I don't even know if you have any."

"I have one of each. And no, they didn't."

"Then why on earth have the piano?"

"I suppose a used upright was the Reader's Digest Condensed Books of their generation."

"But no one played it—so you had to?"

"I had to take lessons. After two and a half years I still didn't play it, and they gave up."

"What a sad story," I said, beginning to laugh.

"The point of which," Charles said, laughing with me, "is that you shouldn't be ashamed because you practiced using the chopsticks."

"You mean you didn't practice?"

"I did. I had to. Mother was there to see to it. But whereas you practiced using chopsticks so that you could do it well, I practiced the piano the way some Catholics practice Catholicism—perfunctorily, and only because it was expected of me. Inside I knew that I really didn't *have* it."

"Given all that, how did you ever come to love music? It must have been an authentic conversion experience."

"You might say. I had an aunt, my father's oldest sister, who was a spinster of fine mind and excellent character, and who had so much leftover love to give, she could have had two dozen nephews and nieces and done well by them all. She was generous with both love and gifts to all those she did have. But I do believe she saved the best for me. I have no idea why I was her favorite, but I was, and I shall always be grateful.

She gave me my first history to read, a dashing version of the life of Henry VIII as a young man—and he *was* dashing then, and learned. And possibly spiritually inclined. Anyway, he was no Charles Laughton caricature, not in the book my aunt gave me. That was my start, I suppose. Wanting to know what made *them*—that Tudor giant and his outlandish daughters—tick.

"Anyway, my aunt taught English in high school. As you can imagine, her income was rather small. Her one personal indulgence was a season ticket to the Metropolitan Opera. The winter before I graduated from high school, she gave me my gift early: she got us tickets, in the first mezzanine, to hear Kirsten Flagstad sing the Ring Cycle.

"It was Flagstad's last Ring. For me, it was . . . well, an initiation into musical pleasure I've never quite recovered from. I suppose taking dope for the first time is like that for some people. And I've heard that some people drink alcoholically from their first teenage beer."

He smiled and said, "I'm just an addict."

"No," I said. "Because the addict will take anything to fill his need. Flagstad and Schiøtz and Horowitz—that's love, not addiction."

"What a nice thing to say," he said. "But speaking of Horowitz, if we don't get going, we'll miss the start."

"That wouldn't be a very loving thing to do," I said. "I'm ready."

Charles signaled for the check, paid it, and we rose to leave. He led the way out, with me following close behind.

As we neared the door another couple, both men, emerging from a different part of the restaurant, arrived at the entranceway just ahead of us. The man in the lead, who was tall, conventionally effeminate and super-stylishly dressed, turned to his companion, about whose appearance there was nothing exceptional—and saw Charles. The tall effeminate man looked at Charles, then behind him to me, then back at Charles, and raised an eyebrow. In the same flamboyant way Douglas Fairbanks used to hoist a petard.

"Hello, Charles," he said. I had a feeling his voice rose and *rose* in pitch at will. At the moment he was unmistakably a countertenor.

"Hello, Harry. How have you been?" It was rhetorical; to emphasize that, Charles turned and motioned to me to keep going.

"More to the point," said Harry, "how have you been?" Having succeeded in stopping our progress, he smiled, then frowned. "I was ever so sorry to hear about dear Ray. It must have been awful, going so suddenly— and for you, of course."

He glanced at me. Then he took the hand of the man he was with, ostensibly only to bring him into the circle of conversation, which so far contained only Charles and Harry, but I knew it was to force Charles to introduce me. "*Excuse* me," he said, handing his companion's hand to Charles, "I don't know if you two know each other."

"No, I'm sorry," Charles said, taking the man's hand.

"Well, that's easily remedied. Perry, this is Charles— a very old friend. Charles and I go way back, don't we, Charles?"

I had the continuing feeling that much of this was for my benefit. I also had a feeling that they didn't go back that far, or that way.

Charles ignored the question. "How do you do," he said to the man called Perry. "Charles Robinson."

"And?" asked Harry coyly.

Charles looked at him.

"We haven't met *your* friend," Harry said, smiling at Charles and then turning it on me intact.

Charles looked at me, and I stepped closer to the men. "Anne," he said, his voice toneless, "this is Harry . . ." It was clear that the man's last name had gone out of his head.

Maybe he'd never known it.

Harry disallowed that possibility by smiling *harder*. "Desmond. Harry Desmond. What traumas can do to our memory!" said Harry, working his smile into false good humor at Charles's lapse of memory. I suppose he doubted it.

"This is Mrs. Durham. Anne Durham," Charles said, going through with it.

"A pleasure to meet you. Any friend of Charles . . . And what a smashing dress! I love it!"

"Thank you," I said.

"This is my friend, Perry Flood."

"Hello," I said, nodding to Perry Flood, who smiled a most reserved smile. I think he felt as awkward as I did. Everyone was uncomfortable except Harry Desmond, who was having a fine time and obviously planned to prolong it.

But Charles cut it short. "Look," he said, "I'm sorry, but we've really got to be going right now. We've tickets and I'm afraid we're on the verge of missing the first piece."

"Oh, by all means, trot on then. I have not forgotten what a music lover you are. Raymond always said you loved music more than . . . well, nearly anything. 'Bye, Mrs. Durham. 'Bye-bye, Charles. Have fun!"

Bastard! "Nice meeting you, Mr. Flood. Goodbye, Mr. Desmond," I said.

Then, deliberately, in slightly slow motion, I took Charles's arm and we walked out of the restaurant. I hung on to his arm until a taxi stopped for us.

Driving to the hall, I couldn't help but feel sorry for that rather shy Mr. Flood. I suspected he had a rather nasty evening in front of him.

Horowitz was . . . Horowitz. But I could feel that Charles was distracted, and that kept me from becoming totally involved in the music. It also angered me.

It always angers me when something keeps me from the music, but this went deeper.

That man in the restaurant, that Harry Desmond, had deliberately attempted to embarrass Charles, to make him squirm. Charles hadn't squirmed, but I was pretty sure he was embarrassed for *me*. I wasn't embarrassed for me, I was embarrassed for *him*. Damn!

I had witnessed a homosexual bitch scene before; I had never before been the impetus for one. Regret over that compounded my anger.

In my ignorance I had blithely assumed that because I was perfectly comfortable going anywhere with Charles, he would be equally comfortable to be seen with me in any circumstances.

Charles, Charles, I *am* sorry.

Tentatively, I touched his arm. He turned toward me. One does not speak, even in a whisper, while Horowitz is playing a late Beethoven sonata, but I tried to tell him, with my eyes, that I wanted very much for him not to miss *this* because of what had happened. Perhaps he read my face accurately. Perhaps he just guessed. He nodded, and looked back toward the stage attentively.

I returned to the music. It was the least I could do if I expected as much of him. When, a few minutes later, at a moment of particularly magical phrasing, I glanced at Charles, he was turning toward me at the same instant, and we met. We had heard it alike. He had been able to listen.

I relaxed then. It was over. It was just an unpleasant incident, and it was over.

Despite the fact that my burgeoning cold was threatening to burst into full bloom at any moment, I thoroughly enjoyed the rest of the concert.

Right on the heels—winged as they were—of Horowitz's last notes, I sneezed. Very loudly.

Charles, applauding, said, "Exquisite timing."

I started clapping too. "Thank you," I said, bowing my head toward Charles. "An accolade it would be falsely humble to reject."

Leaving the hall, I felt a bit uncertain on my feet. Without thinking this time, I took Charles's arm. This time he pressed my hand against his side. "Hang on," he said, and got us through the crowd with an efficiency that reminded me of Philip . . . Anderway.

Philip Anderway. I hadn't thought of him in a long time. Now, reflexively, I glanced around at the departing crowd. If he could, he would be there. But I didn't see him.

I must admit I didn't look very hard.

When we emerged from the concert hall into the

breezy night, I was sweating from the press of people
—or from a fever. It was hard at that moment to tell
which it was. It hardly mattered. I felt awful, fever or no.

On the outer steps, Charles let go my arm and
turned to me. He frowned. "You look flushed," he said.
"Do you want to go somewhere and sit down? A coffee
house? A bar?"

"Honest?"

"I should think so," he said in that professorial tone
he seldom used.

"All right. What I'd like is a taxi—the first available
taxi. Please. I think I feel the plague coming on."

Without another word, he got us a taxi—the first
one, as a matter of fact.

18

COME MORNING, there was no longer any question about
it. Plague it was. I felt rotten through and through.

I looked at the bedside clock. It read ten forty-five.
I must have turned off the alarm and gone back to sleep,
or never pulled it out last night at all. I couldn't remember which.

It didn't much matter; when I tried to get out of
bed, I discovered I wasn't up to it. My neck was stiff,
my back ached, my muscles throbbed. I gave up and
lay back.

With most of the energy at my command, I pulled the phone to the edge of the night table and lifted it onto my stomach. I dialed the shop.

"Hello." Munch didn't sound in the least frantic.

"It's me."

"Hello?"

"It's me!"

"Are you sure?"

If I could have laughed, I would have. "Not absolutely. Check. If I'm there instead of here, hang up gently and call Bellevue. The address is Twenty-four West Seventy-fourth Street."

"Are you all right?"

"Of course not. Would I be advising you to call Bellevue if I weren't crazy enough to think I might be there?"

"You've got a *terrible* cold."

"I gather you've checked and I'm not there."

"Anne, be serious. You're *sick*."

"Win one, you lose one."

"You're not making sense."

"Let's start over. Munch, this is Anne. I don't think I'll be in this morning. You see, I have this terrible cold."

"You sound awful—like Robert Mitchum."

"Not Tallulah Bankhead?" I've always had a yen to sound like Tallulah Bankhead.

"What's your temperature?"

"I don't know. Why?"

"You sound like a hundred and three."

"I thought I sounded like Robert Mitchum."

"You do. Like Robert Mitchum with a hundred and three."

"You're very funny."

"You're *sick*. Listen, take your temperature, stay in bed, take two aspirin every four hours, and drink plenty of liquids."

"You forgot to tell me to gargle."

"Don't you know enough to gargle when you've got a cold?"

"You are funny."

"Pneumonia isn't. Now get off this phone and *rest*. Better yet, sleep. I'll call you later."

She hung up. I put the phone on the floor and made another stab at getting out of bed. With what struck me as immoderate effort for a woman who takes exercise classes regularly, I finally made it to my feet.

I gargled, holding on to the bathroom sink with one hand to steady myself. I took two aspirin out of the bottle in the medicine cabinet and went into the kitchen for some juice, an expedition which should have earned me a small medal, I felt.

There was half a container of orange juice in the refrigerator. I swallowed the aspirin and drank all the juice.

I made my way back to the bathroom and then returned to bed, clutching a thermometer.

Three minutes or so later I knew I had a hundred and two point eight.

I wouldn't have told Munch for anything, but I sure felt like a hundred and three.

The ringing of the phone woke me. At first I thought the ringing was inside my head. I located it on the fifth ring and pulled it up on the bed.

As I picked up the receiver I checked the bedside

clock. It was noon. How was I going to get rested if Munch kept checking on whether I was resting?

"It was only a hundred and two," I lied slightly. "And *no,* I have not taken it again since I took the aspirin."

"That is real fever for an adult, isn't it?"

"Charles! I'm sorry, I thought it was Munch—my partner?"

"I remember."

"Yes, well, she's been doctoring me by telephone."

"I won't keep you. I just want to know if there's anything you need—aspirin, juices . . ."

"Thanks, but Munch will stop by later and she can—"

"I'm closer," he said. "And available now. I have no classes on Monday."

"Has anyone ever told you that you're doggedly reasonable, and in my condition I'm in no condition— Yes, I'd love some juice."

"What kinds do you like?"

"Since I can't taste anything anyway, I wouldn't be able to tell except by color. I drank the last ounce of juice in the house with my breakfast aspirin."

"How would a chilled bottle of grapefruit juice do for a start? I have one in the refrigerator."

"Ugh! That sounds revoltingly healthy. Bring on the grapefruit juice."

"I'll be right there," he said, and hung up.

I got myself out of bed and my arms into a robe, and staggered to the door.

"Are you there?" I asked.

"Naturally," he said.

I opened the door. "You didn't ring."

He rang. "Okay? Here," he said, holding out the bottle to me. I took it.

And he was gone.

I shut the door. God, I must look even worse than I feel. No. As bad. I couldn't look worse.

The bottle weighed at least twenty pounds. I carried it into the kitchen, opened it, drank two glasses so I wouldn't have to get out of bed again for a week, put the bottle in the refrigerator, and wended my way back to bed.

It was the phone which awakened me again. My throat felt like an emery board.

I got hold of the receiver. "Umn hmn," I said.

"Feeling lousy, huh," Munch said.

"Umn hmn."

"What should I bring? I'm coming over on my way home."

"I'm not on your way home."

"Tonight you will be."

"Besides, I don't need anything. And, dear sweet heart, I love you for wanting to, but I don't feel like company, even you. Thanks, anyway."

"Wasn't planning on staying. You sound as contagious as the plague."

"Which is only appropriate."

"Now hear this. You are not suffering from anything but a bad cold and a concomitant bad temper. I wouldn't dream of paying a social call on anyone in that condition. Just regard me as a simple delivery man. You couldn't possibly have everything you need."

"Wrong. As it happens, I have everything in the

entire world I need, except my health. If you come across it, by all means bring it by. As for my distemper, may I point out that I have recently—in the past twenty-four hours, as a matter of fact—begun a research study which already shows that there is something worse than having a terminal illness. And that is feeling so stinking you wish your illness were terminal."

"Talk to you later," said Munch tranquilly.

"It's not the best thing for my voice, which is fading, lest you hadn't noticed."

"You don't have to talk. I'll talk to you," she said.

"Umn hmn," I said, because it was short, mainly, and hung up.

As I was trying to move the phone back up on the table, it rang again.

"What I really need, Munch, is *rest*."

"I'm sorry," said Charles. "And you're absolutely right, that is what you need most of. But if you'll just come to the door once more, you'll find something else you could use, I think. I promise not to bother you again today, but I'll be here, so if you need anything, you call *me*. Hear?"

"Yes, sir. And thank you. I'll remember. Goodbye."

I hung up, and lay back. If I need anything, call Charles. That was nice of him. There was something else. Something I had to do.

I had to sleep.

When the phone rang the next time, I was half-awake, coming slowly out of a deep sleep and seriously considering whether it was worth making the effort to get to the bathroom in order to gargle. My throat felt so rough, it might have been transformed from an emery board to industrial-grade sandpaper while I slept. My head felt hot. In fact, my whole body felt hot. Two aspirin were in order.

But first the phone, which was still ringing. I reached for it, and my hand knocked over a half-filled glass of water I had left on my bedside table.

"Hello!"

"You're still angry with me."

"What! Oh, it's you, David. No, I'm not angry at you. I just spilled something reaching for the phone."

"Good!" he said.

"Good! It's all over the carpet," I said.

"I'm sorry about the spillage. I wish I were there to sponge it up, really. I just meant I was glad you're not angry at me any more. I knew, when I called, and you sounded so cool and calm, that you must have been fuming. Anyway, it's past, and I'm grateful. I promised to let you know my schedule as soon as I knew it myself. It's just been finalized. I'll be in next Monday. My plane gets in at four-forty. Have dinner with me?"

"I really don't have much of an appetite these days," I said. Or voice, David.

"You will in a week," he said cheerfully. "Got to run to a meeting. I'm already late. But I did want to let you know when we'd be together again. Goodbye, darling."

He'd hung up! "Don't I even sound like a bad connection!" I shouted into the dead receiver in my hand.

Just what my throat needed.

I got out of bed, feeling woozy, and went into the kitchen for a roll of paper toweling. In the bedroom, I found I couldn't lean over that far without getting very dizzy, so I got down on my hands and knees and patted away at the carpet.

Then I sat back on the bed and rested a few minutes. There seemed no point in getting back in bed until I had medicated this damned cold as best I could. I got myself to the bathroom, gargled, and took two aspirin into the kitchen, where I downed them with another glass of the grapefruit juice.

Done in entirely by this expedition, I returned to bed to be sick in the seemliest position, supine. Thanks to David's call, I was now feeling assaulted even in the one muscle my cold had not reached: my heart felt black and blue.

I felt mad and hurt and miserable. All day everyone had been saying I sounded awful. Was one of David's ears plugged with self-preoccupation and the other with caution? How are you, Anne? Anne, how's everything? Anne, your voice sounds funny, you okay? I tried out various possibilities, any one of which would have elicited the information that I was *ill*. Everyone was interested in my deteriorated physical condition except David. Everyone was solicitous except David. Everyone —Dear God! Charles! The call! The door! That's what I was supposed to do. I had fallen asleep again without fetching in whatever was at the door.

I dragged myself out of bed, weighed down by self-pity, and walked as though through water to the door.

Outside, on a tray, stood a full, covered pitcher of orange juice, and numerous cans of juices of various denominations, from orthodox tomato to evangelical papaya. I bent to the tray, grasping the side of the door for support. I knelt there for a moment, staring, deciding whether to fight back the tears which were on their way.

Too exhausting just then, I decided. I needed all my strength to get everything into the house. Two by two I carried the cans into the kitchen. Then, when just the pitcher of orange juice was left, I lifted the tray and carried it into the bedroom.

I got me into bed, with the tray on my lap, and poured some of the orange juice into the glass on the bedside table.

It was! It was real live orange juice. Not the kind that comes out of cans or containers, but the kind that comes out of oranges. The kind my mother used to squeeze for me when I was sick. I didn't mind that it wasn't cold. I didn't even care if all the vitamins had escaped in the hours I had left it outside my door. It was the most delicious damned juice I'd ever tasted.

David Meray, I know what you would do if you were here—and noticed that I had a lulu of a cold. You would bring me a big bouquet of flowers, and maybe, maybe, if you were really inspired, you would go into a restaurant and ask them to sell you a quart or a half-gallon or even a gallon of fresh orange juice. They'd say yes, and charge you five dollars, and bring you orange juice they'd transferred from one container to a plain one, and you wouldn't know the difference.

You wouldn't know the difference.

I took a swig of the orange juice as my tears began to dilute it.

19

HAVING FINISHED THE ENTIRE PITCHER of orange juice, I spent a fitful night. I had to get up twice to go to the bathroom, and both times I returned to the same dream when I went back to sleep again. I know some people claim they can do that when they want to, but I've never been able to. I certainly didn't want to get back into this dream. David was in there, playing several parts, none of them heroic.

Waking, I realized that I could not at that moment do anything about how I felt about David, but I had better do something about my body. My head felt hot, I was sweating, and my muscles ached as if I'd developed dystrophy overnight. My throat no longer felt like industrial sandpaper; it had gone back to that emery-board sensation. But now my nose was stuffed. I reached for a tissue and blew into it. Nothing.

Altogether, it was clear that my cold wasn't just passing through; it had moved in on me for a while. I roused myself and was gargling in the bathroom when the phone rang.

It's not David. He does not know you are sick. He would not expect to find you home at this hour.

It wasn't David. Disappointment shot through me.

"I didn't wake you? Are you any better? Did you sleep? Can I do anything for you?" Munch recited her questions the way a six-year-old recites poetry, hurtling toward the end.

"What if this was a wrong number?" I asked, my disappointment abating because Munch did know and care and not everybody has somebody to care. Besides, she was funny.

"Hello. Is this Mrs. Durham's apartment? If it happens to be, may I speak with her, please?"

"Munch, you're the eighth wonder. No. Not much. Some. What was the last question?"

"What were the first three? *I'm* a wonder. How can you remember questions I asked half a conversation ago. I just wanted to know—how are you?"

"I suspect I'll live, although I'm not altogether certain that's good news."

"How come?"

"David called last night and he didn't ask how I was."

"He didn't know you were sick."

"He still doesn't."

"You mean he couldn't tell from your voice?"

"If he could, I couldn't tell from *his* voice."

"Shit!" said Munch, who didn't often resort to basic English.

"Thank God! I was beginning to think I was hallucinating that I had reason to be slightly put out by that."

"Were you able to sleep?"

"Yes, I slept on and off. When I slept, that was kind of off, too. I dreamt about David."

"You shouldn't have. Listen, love, can I get you anything?"

"Uh uh. Thanks, though. I've got aspirin, salt for gargling, liquids to liquefy my brain. Ugh! Leprosy must have a more interesting course of treatment. You know what else they can't cure besides the common cold?"

"A broken heart."

"How'd you guess?"

"You're feeling sorry for yourself in flashy primary colors, that's how. Check again. Is your heart broken, I mean *broken*, sweetheart? Or maybe only dented?"

I checked it out. I didn't say anything.

After a moment Munch said, "Don't feel deprived. You may get another chance, but this time you'll live."

Suddenly, I felt a little better. My heart wasn't broken. Why on earth that made me feel *better* was beyond me. I mean, discovering you care less about a person than you thought you did, that's a terrible discovery, isn't it?

"Munch, you're a friend."

"Terrific. Look, you must be out of juice by now. I'll pick some up—"

"No. Thanks, really. I've got plenty." I tried to remember some of the labels on the cans. I couldn't, so I improvised. "Apricot, cranberry, cranapple, pear . . ."

"Since when have you become a juice freak? It wouldn't have occurred to me to bring anything but grapefruit or orange. Have you been having a thing on the side with the market delivery boy?"

I laughed. "Not on the side or in any other position. He's about sixty-eight and has warts. Charles brought the juices."

"Oh."

"You know what, Munch? He squeezed a whole pitcher of fresh orange juice for me."

"Charles Robinson squeezed a pitcher of orange juice for you." A pause. "I guess if he felt like it, that's okay. At least you're safe with him. You never know about delivery boys. Warts don't make a man impotent, you know."

"The way I look, I'd be safe with the Boston strangler."

"Good. Listen, you'll call me if you need *anything?* *I* haven't squeezed fresh orange juice in twenty years, but for you . . . And we deliver all hours, remember?"

"I remember. And I'll call, I promise. If I need anything."

"Goodbye."

"Goodbye. And thanks for making me check to see if my heart was really broken, and"—I spoke very gently—"for being a little jealous because Charles squeezed me juice."

"I don't know what you're talking about," Munch said, "but you're probably still running a fever and I forgive you."

She hung up.

I did the same and returned to the bathroom. The salt water had turned tepid. I started over again, with more salt and hot water. The phone rang.

"Hello!"

"I guess I've called at a bad time. I'm sorry," said Charles. "I'll call back later."

"No, it's all right. *I'm* sorry. It's just that I was gargling and Munch called and the gargle got cold and I just made another one and the phone rang again and I thought it was Munch again."

He was laughing, but I didn't mind. Come to think of it, he had been sounding better the past few days. Maybe he was beginning to feel himself again, and the hurt was getting duller. Maybe I was just reading too much into the fact that I had said something that sounded funny and he had laughed.

"There's a fresh pitcher of juice outside your door,"

Charles said matter-of-factly, as if this were a daily arrangement of long standing.

"Now, how on earth did you know I finished the entire pitcher you left yesterday?"

"I just know I squeeze a mean glass of orange juice and you wouldn't be able to resist. Feeling any better at all?"

"You know, I think I am." I was—a little. Two mouthfuls of gargle and some of the tightness was gone. Somewhere.

"Good. I'll speak to you when I get home from my classes. Meanwhile, take care. Goodbye."

Hey, wait!

I didn't say it, but I had thought of saying it. Very slowly I replaced the receiver, and I think I smiled.

I must have smiled. Because my lip split.

The next time he called I was sitting up in bed, reading the Doris Lessing novel I'd started unsuccessfully weeks earlier, and sipping a glass of orange juice.

"Hello?"

"I didn't wake you, good."

"I'm reading. And turning orange, I suspect, thanks to you."

"As long as it doesn't come out in blotches," he said.

"Blotches! I've never had a blotch in my life!"

"You are feeling a little better, aren't you?"

"I am."

"Nonetheless, you mustn't stop doing the right things yet. You sound awfully nasal."

"You say the sweetest things."

"It's not a criticism," he said evenly. "It's a statement of fact."

"Umn."

He laughed. "You're not going to inveigle me into apologizing because *your* cold's gone to *your* nose. I do have something for you, and if you don't come to the door, it will get cold—it must be taken hot."

"Taken? It's medicine? There isn't any medicine for a cold, everybody knows that."

"Are you coming to the door, or aren't you?"

"That's a *walk*! Tell me what it is first."

"It's for your cold. Just believe me."

I thought. "Is it herb tea? I like herb tea."

"Anne, come to the door." Professor Robinson speaking.

"I'm coming. I'm coming."

I hung up and got out of bed and into a robe. I decided to stop in the bathroom on the way to the door. I didn't want to scare the man. I brushed at my hair, two swipes. I reached for a lipstick, opened it, swiveled it, and moved in on the mirror to apply it. Orange? I was grey-beige. Sort of a pale taupe. I put down the lipstick (it wouldn't help) and went to the door.

Opening it, I faced a smiling Charles holding a tray containing a bowl of . . . chicken soup.

I stared at it, and then at him. "You have a lot of trays," I said, because I couldn't for the moment think of anything else to say. Making chicken soup is work.

Then I said, "I didn't know you were Jewish." Very aptly put.

"I'm not," he said. "But it's authentic, *and* it's getting heavy to hold. So do please take it and eat it. Now."

His tone was stern but his eyes were the opposite. I got the feeling he was very pleased with himself. "There's more for tomorrow."

"Yes, sir," I said, and took the tray.

Immediately, he turned toward his own apartment.

"Hey," I called. "Thanks!"

"It's getting cold." He shut his door.

20

IT MUST HAVE BEEN THAT SOUP. I am not the world's foremost connoisseur of chicken soup, lacking the requisite genes, but Charles's chicken soup must have contained the exact proportions of appropriate magical properties. The following morning my nose began to run productively, my throat felt lined only with human tissue, my temperature was normal, and despite a few remaining aches and pains, I began to wonder how my plants were surviving the illness in the house.

I was making a remarkable recovery, considering.

Considering David.

Considering Charles, too. A friend in need cuts a cold in half. It might not be worth immortalizing in needlework, but it was a comforting thought. A comfortable thought.

I got out of bed, put on a robe, and looked over the damage to my plants. Given the midsummer sun, it was not surprising that all but my cacti sorely needed watering. My lovely large coleus, grown from a friend's cutting, drooped unto despair—mine, that it might be too far gone to come back. I filled the watering can and gave the coleus as much water as it could take, then started on the other plants. I had to fill my watering can four times. Then I misted all of those that like misting.

Tentatively, I approached the coleus again. It had happened, that tiny miracle you mustn't count on happening too many times: recovery was visible to the eye. I sat down on the sofa, to rest and watch my coleus pull itself upright again. It was a beautiful thing to see.

A bit rested, and very relieved, I addressed my green friends. "I just want you to know that I think it was damn decent of all of you to bear with being totally ignored the past two days. You are stalwart, each and every one of you. I love you all. What's more, I like you. And I'll tell you why. You're *here*."

Like Charles.

I wondered how Charles would feel about being compared with my plants, and decided he would probably take it in stride.

That afternoon Charles appeared with another bowl of soup. This time there was a chicken leg plunk in the middle of the bowl.

In the evening he brought me a homemade banana split.

"For energy," he said.

I hadn't eaten a banana split since high school. They're good.

The following morning there were definite signs that I was edging into myself again. Mainly I looked worse than I felt, and I *cared*.

In the afternoon Charles called me from the college and I reported my condition accurately, except that I skipped mentioning how bad I looked. He'd seen me the past three days, and he didn't wear glasses.

He said he'd be over at dinnertime.

"I'd like that," I said, "I really would. I'm feeling like some human company. I guess that means I'm feeling human again. But I'm afraid I'm not up to cooking—"

"Well, of course not. I cooked our dinner last night. It'll only need warming and I'll do that before I bring it over."

"Now, wait a minute. How did you know I'd be up to eating real food today?"

"I'm an historian, remember? The history of colds told me you would be."

"But colds last a week. I've only had this one four days."

"History is the story of exceptions."

"And exceptional men and women, right?"

"Right." No more.

"I was fishing for a compliment," I said.

"Yes, you are," he said. "Anne, a student of mine just came in. We've an appointment. I'll be over around six. Meanwhile, take a nap. You need a lot of rest still." He hung up.

Bossy.

Very nice bossy.

I took a nap—bits and pieces of a nap, anyway. I kept thinking I'd better check the time, in case a whole hunk of it had sneaked by me, but when I'd look, it would never be more than five or ten minutes since the last reading. I found that moderately perplexing. I usually have a better sense of time than that.

At four I decided that a bath would make me feel better. Cleaner, certainly.

I ran a tub and soaked in the well-oiled water for ten minutes. Then I quickly dried myself and got back under the covers.

And thought.

Nothing earth-shaking. Not even anything consecutive.

I did notice something about my thinking that was new.

For the past few days I had spent a good part of my waking hours drinking Charles's orange juice and eating Charles's chicken soup, and feeling resentful toward David.

What I found myself thinking now was—it was not so unusual, David's behavior; what was unusual was Charles's behavior.

He was really being exceptionally nice to me.

And that was nice—not just because it was uncomplicated, either.

.   .   .

At five I decided that the least I could do toward dinner was my face. It took a bit of doing.

When Charles arrived I was waiting for his ring in the living room, wearing a fresh, rosy robe, and if I didn't look good, I didn't look oppressively bad.

As I waited it had bothered me that I didn't feel in the least hungry. I had had the last of the chicken soup for lunch, and eaten every bit of the meat in it. It had probably been too much.

He had gone to all this trouble. I would have to eat some of it, I told myself. But as soon as I let him in, the lemony smell escaping from the steaming covered dish he carried resurrected my appetite. Dinner was a deceptively simple baked chicken on rice in lemon sauce.

Lovely. Just to taste again.

After we ate, Charles put on a record for me to listen to. So I wouldn't fidget while he cleaned up our few dishes, he explained. The record he chose was the Cantata #1 by Bach, the masterful Archive recording of that relentlessly restorative work. He was back before it was half through, and sat across from me and listened with me until the end.

And then he was going.

Too soon.

"Do you play Scrabble?" I asked.

"I am a past master of the game, madam," he said, poker-faced.

"Are you now? Well, I'm a pretty snazzy player myself, I'll have you know. And I'd like to take you on—that is, if you've no plans for the next hour."

"In your weakened condition, I think a game

between us would involve my taking unfair advantage
—which I don't happen to require."

"Dinner at the Coach House, loser's treat," I said
in my most businesslike voice. Mr. Shapley would have
succumbed to that tone immediately.

Charles was thinking it over.

Stay. Please stay.

"All right, we'll play," he said. "One game. Then
you must go to bed. I don't want you getting overtired
and having a relapse. But not for any stakes. It just
wouldn't be fair."

He really was cocky, however nicely he put it.

"Don't overestimate yourself," I said. "Dinner at
the Coach House."

He looked at me levelly for a moment. I was sure
he was going to refuse. "Dinner at the Coach House,"
he said. "As it happens, one of my favorite eateries."

"Good," I said. "It's settled, then."

I told him where the set, a pad and a pencil were,
and he set the game up.

And he won.

But not by all that much. Not when you consider
my weakened condition.

It was fun playing against such a good player. And
a good winner, to boot.

"The Coach House," he said as he left, "on the lady
who came close."

The next evening Charles arrived, after phoning in
the afternoon to check on my progress, bearing a superb
poached bass and a chilled bottle of Pouilly-Fumé.

I felt well enough to be wearing that new caftan I'd bought. My color wasn't ready for a *Vogue* cover, but it was coming along.

The bass was delicious. As was the Pouilly-Fumé. But my mouth was watering for our return Scrabble match, which I had, that afternoon, set as a condition for his cooking dinner again.

Halfway through our game Charles said, "You really are feeling better this evening."

"Because you're not winning?" I answered glibly and without looking up because it was my turn.

"No," he said in a voice that made me look up—too late.

I felt I had missed something. No. I would not be distracted by outguessing games. I concentrated on the game at hand.

Which Charles ended up winning anyway, by seven lousy points.

I now owed him dinner at the Coach House and my secret chili recipe.

I didn't mind as much as I thought I would.

On Sunday, Charles said it was time I went out, and he took me for a walk in the park. It was a brilliant tangerine-sun day and it felt good to be out, but we didn't really walk very far. I tired rather quickly, whereupon Charles expeditiously selected a good bench for us to sit on. It had an exceptional view and we had it all to ourselves.

We sat quietly. I could feel my body virtually suck in the sunshine, the way a thirsty plant sucks in water. He had been right; it was doing me good to be out.

In a while, just when I was beginning to feel that I had had enough, he said it was time to go home.

Where he prepared a zucchini omelet for us.

We listened to the trio at the end of *Der Rosenkavalier*, the Schwarzkopf-Edelman-Ludwig recording with Von Karajan conducting. I cried a little, and Charles smiled at me, and when it was over, we didn't either of us talk about how marvelous it was.

A little later he went home, and I went to bed.

In the morning I decided against going in to the shop, although I was feeling up to at least half a day's work.

I had some thinking to do. Hard thinking.

And for the first time in days I felt up to it.

21

WHEN DAVID TELEPHONED from the airport, I agreed to have dinner with him. He said he'd pick me up at seven. He sounded in excellent spirits.

I dressed with care. Sitting in the sun the previous day had done much to restore my color, but I played it safe and wore red. With only a smidgen more rouge than usual, my face showed no sign that only days before, it had been a sedate, elegant—deadly—taupe.

I was downstairs waiting when his taxi pulled up.

He took me to The Four Seasons, where he insisted on ordering champagne. When it arrived, he toasted me, saying that I looked particularly beautiful. Then he explained his extraordinary good humor.

"I've arranged to have an entire week in the city in September," he said. "We can be together every evening. A whole week of evenings." His pleasure at the prospect was obvious. He really relished the idea of a whole week of evenings spent with me.

Did I, with him?

There it was, a line near the bottom.

I suddenly knew why I had fussed so over my appearance. It was in order to obviate any possibility that David's eyes would now guess what his ears had missed. I realized that I had no intention of telling him I'd been sick. Not about my cold, nor my anger, nor my hurt.

There was no point.

The line near the bottom became the bottom line: there was no point to David and me any longer.

I had decided that afternoon. Not quickly and not positively.

Now, sitting across a candlelit table from him, sipping good champagne, my gut, in an instant, was sure.

A week of evenings with David meant dinners in expensive restaurants, good seats to the second-best show in town, and enjoyable sex. I had not forgotten the day we looked out over the Hudson from the Cloisters, walked happily through Chinatown, and rode twice back and forth on the Staten Island ferry. But I knew now—I didn't know how, but I knew—that that day was a day out of tune. It was a day David designed . . .

for me—a day made of gossamer . . . the unhardy stuff of romance. It didn't have anything to do with everyday life.

A week of evenings with David seemed too long to me.

I didn't say that to him. I wouldn't. Right then, I only said I wanted to get home early, I was tired.

"You don't look tired," he said, smiling. But he didn't probe, and he tried not to look disappointed. I guess he had that week of his to look forward to.

In the taxi going home, he said he'd be here until Thursday morning. When could he see me Tuesday?

"I don't think I can make it Tuesday," I said.

He didn't say anything, but he turned to look at me. I looked at him—it was the least I could do.

"I can't make it Wednesday, either. Or in September."

"There's someone else," he said.

A man with a healthy ego. What other reason could there be for ending a relationship with him than that there was someone new in my life.

I didn't answer.

"Is there someone else?" He was beginning to sound as if he could get nasty.

Still, a question deserves an answer. "Yes," I said. "Me."

The taxi pulled up in front of my house. I sat there for a moment, politely, in case there was anything he wanted to say, but he didn't. I got out.

"Goodbye, David," I said, bending slightly as I began to close the taxi door.

He put his hand out then, to hold the door open. "You might have told me over the phone, when I called to say I was coming in," he said. His voice was petulant, complaining, almost whining. "I went to a great deal of trouble, you know. It took some doing. I had to *arrange* things. Actually"—he poked his head out of the cab and brought it so close to my face, we were almost touching—"you could probably have told me when I called last week. I can tell, you didn't just decide this. So that would have been the decent thing to do. You really should have told me then, Anne."

"Maybe you're right, but it was a poor connection," I said.

And left him.

22

TUESDAY MORNING I felt glad.

Glad to be back in the shop, feeling myself again. Glad to have it over with with David, feeling myself again that way too.

I told Munch.

She asked if I had broken up with David because of someone else.

I did not say to her, as I had said to David, "Yes, me." I said, "You know there's no one else."

And she said, "I just thought I'd ask," and showed me the figures for the week I'd been out.

I thought it prudent to skip my exercise class that night. Prudence comes very low on my personal list of *good* virtues, but there is something to be said for occasional recourse to it. I ate a light supper Tuesday night and was in bed by nine o'clock.

Wednesday morning I felt so fit, I called Alex. She hadn't called me since before my cold, and I never call her when I'm not up to snuff, so we had been out of touch long enough for me to suspect she and Tom might be having at it again. I asked if the two of them would like to join me for supper out that evening and Shakespeare in the Park, my treat. She said that sounded nice, could she check with Tom and get back to me.

She called back in a few minutes and said they'd love to.

We met at a restaurant called Serendipity, and they bickered from the terrific cheezy crackers to the slightly too-rich fudge pie. I felt remarkably detached.

During *Romeo and Juliet*, Alex laughed a few times. Tom tried to shush her and—I could swear she grabbed his arm and gave him an Indian burn.

I thought it was a poor performance.

Romeo and Juliet was fine.

Thursday, I made three good sales—which is not Thursday kind of business—and I returned to my exercise class.

Friday night Charles and I went to the Coach House. Charles wore a white linen jacket. I wore a white linen dress with a full pleated skirt and high-heeled white sandals. We granted that we each looked marvelous.

The evening was a real kick.

The antebellum service, which sometimes gnawed at my liberal predilections, amused me. The black bean soup was divine. The chocolate cake was sinfully rich. The wine was first-rate—and ridiculously overpriced.

Graciousness and gustatory delights: a once-a-year (and once-a-year-is-enough) evening.

Charles didn't insist on paying. I didn't insist on actually paying the check with my own two hands—I passed him three twenties under the table. I suppose it was the Southernness rubbing off on us both.

Afterward we walked a ways up Fifth Avenue. I told Charles I had just ended a relationship.

"The man I saw you with one Sunday morning?" He remembered David.

I nodded.

"A handsome man," he said.

"He had a space between his two front teeth," I said, for no reason.

"That wasn't why you stopped seeing him," Charles said.

"No," I said. "It was why I started seeing him, I think."

"He seemed nice at a glance."

"He was nice enough." No, not quite nice enough. "Anyway, it's over."

"I'm sorry," he said.

"Don't be," I said. "I'm not."

"Then I'm not," he said.

Enough. "Let's go to my place and I'll make you the best daiquiri you ever tasted," I said.

"After *that* chocolate cake?"

"Why not?" I said. "We're celebrating, aren't we?"

"Always," he said, laughing lightly. "But what particular earthshaking felicitousness are we celebrating tonight?"

"My excellent health," I said. "A sound mind in a sound body."

"In an honest-to-God glamorous dress. It almost does you justice," he said.

"You're very gallant."

"No, I'm not," he said. Convincingly. He flagged a passing taxi. "Let's go have that daiquiri," he said.

The next week I presented Charles with the chili receipe I owed him, stuck in a big pot of chili.

We ate it together.

It took us four evenings.

It didn't get boring.

The following Sunday it rained. We scoured the *Times*, made a list of three movies we could see consecutively that afternoon. It meant we had to run four blocks in five minutes between the second and third films, but we made it.

Two of the films were fine, one was awful.

Feeling like winners, we decided on a Scrabble tournament, to be held at once, and hurried home. I made us scrambled eggs while Charles set up the first game. We played three.

Charles won the first one.

I won the second.

The third, I won by two points.

We had forgotten to decide on the winner's prize.

"I'll think of something," Charles said. "Willing to leave it up to me?"

"Yes."

It took him a week. Then he presented me with an envelope containing two tickets to every single film at the upcoming festival at Lincoln Center.

"Does that mean I can go with whomever I choose?" I asked.

"Of course," he said.

"Oh, good," I said.

On the Saturday of Labor Day weekend we went to the beach.

I wore my lavender-and-green near-bikini. Charles wore conservative navy trunks. He has a nice body.

It was fifty degrees out. We both went in.

Late that night Munch happened to call, and I told her. She said we were crazy.

The way she said it, she'd been waiting for weeks to say it.

"Could be," I said.

Alex had called to invite me to Sunday brunch. I didn't feel up to being a spectator at a prolonged bickering match again. As a preventive measure, I asked if I could bring a friend.

Alex said sure. She didn't ask who.

I asked Charles if he was willing to help me out of what I regarded as a maternal bind.

"Sure," he said. "But as I recall, your daughter doesn't take to strangers."

I had forgotten that Saturday when Alex and I had met Charles and Raymond, and I had introduced them. Apparently, Charles had been alert to Alex's frosty disapproval. He was right, of course, I couldn't ask him to go with me.

"Don't misunderstand," he said, "I'm perfectly willing to go with you. I just thought I ought to mention it, in case you'd forgotten we'd already met."

"I had, and I'm sorry. Forget it."

"If that's the way you want it," Charles said.

"Thanks anyway," I said.

Fifteen minutes later I called him back. "I just can't face them alone. If you're really willing to come . . ."

"It's settled," he said.

We went.

We stayed nearly two hours.

It was really very funny. For one thing, it worked: Alex and Tom were civil to each other the entire time. And it was evident from the moment we walked in, that my daughter didn't remember ever having met Charles.

Needless to say, we did not remind her. We laughed about that together on the way home.

On Labor Day itself, it was warm and sunny and clear. Charles suggested a walk in the park. If he hadn't, I would have. It was a perfect day for it.

For hours we walked.

Eventually, after a long, long time, exhaustion came upon us. Fortunately, we found an unoccupied bench nearby and sat.

For a while then we leaned back and soaked in the sun, not speaking. I began to feel drowsy from the combination of walking and sunning, and my eyes were not completely focused on the man as he walked in our direction. He was alone, a thin blond young man, wearing jeans and a tank top. He walked slowly, sort of sauntering along. He was almost in front of us when he seemed to slow down discernibly, almost stop. Then he shrugged and walked on.

I turned to Charles, squinting to see him clearly in the sun. "He knew you," I said.

Charles didn't say anything.

"You did know him, didn't you?" I persisted.

"Yes," he said. "Briefly." The words came out stingily.

"He stopped. Why didn't you say hello to him? It's not like you to be rude."

"Look." He sounded tired, more than the long walk would account for. "I just wanted to avoid a repetition of that scene in the Japanese restaurant the night we went to hear Horowitz. You haven't forgotten that pleasant little scene with Harry Desmond, have you?"

"I thought that might be it," I said. "Charles, I'm sorry that at times my presence seems to cause you embarrassment."

"Of course I was embarrassed! But not for me." He sounded as if I were slow.

"For me? Charles, I don't know exactly how to put this, but I have a rather high embarrassment threshold."

"Perhaps you do. But if it's like having a high pain threshold, eventually you feel it, just like everybody else. Just as intensely as anyone else."

"It may work like that. I don't know," I said.

"Exactly," said Charles.

There wasn't anything I could say to that. I didn't know. He was right.

And looked so unhappy to be.

"How sad you look," I said.

"That's foolish on such a lovely day, isn't it?" he said, and sort of smiled. For a man who smiled often and easily . . . it looked like work.

"Oh, Charles . . ." Without thinking, I put my hand on his, which were clasped tightly in his lap. He looked down at my hand as if it required his attention. Except for the time I had pointedly taken his arm, when we were leaving the Japanese restaurant under the dubious eye of that Harry, I had found myself restraining my customary tactileness. Not blatantly, I hoped, the way some people speak loudly to foreigners, but I felt that a certain reticence would keep things comfortable for us both.

But now there it was, my hand, and he was looking at it—attentively. Taking it back now would be such an italicized movement. I left it where it was.

"Charles," I said, feeling my way, "you've been so kind to me—so good for me these past weeks—I just can't tell you. Kids make friends easily . . . and lightly. Not now. Not me, anyway. And now I see you sad and I know I've brought it on somehow. Charles, I can't bear your sadness, even if it isn't exactly my fault. There must be something I can do . . ."

"I've been good for *you*," he said, his voice tight. "Do you—can you—realize what it's been like for me to laugh again? To do something spontaneously, to feel myself alive again—even to squeeze orange juice for someone. You think of that juice as something *I* did for you . . ." He shook his head incredulously.

"But if it—all of it—ends up making you sad . . ."

Abruptly, Charles got up. I thought, He's going to walk away from me. But he stood there, waiting, and

I got up, too, and we began to walk. His head down, he set a slow pace.

Slowly, he talked, an unexpected clinical tone to his voice. "Anne, I lived with Raymond for six years. We were very different—but it was, I think, a good relationship. We complemented each other. We really enjoyed each other's company. And we filled . . . certain needs for each other—not all of them sexual. It was an honest relationship."

He shook his head then, as if he weren't saying it accurately, after all.

"Charles, don't you know that you don't have to tell me anything about Raymond?"

"I think I do have to say it," he said in that stern voice he used so seldom.

"All right." I gave in. "You can tell me anything you want to. I only want you to realize that . . . Charles, I *know* what it feels like to be married—and widowed."

He stopped walking and faced me. "You know more than one would hope for, I'll admit that. Anne, how did you become a translator of the heart?"

It was an astonishing thing to say, and I had no idea how to reply. If what he said had truth in it, I was grateful, but I felt he was *too* grateful for what understanding I could bring to his bereavement. After all, I had been there.

Not knowing what to say, I said nothing. I started to walk again and he kept step beside me.

I don't know how long we walked like that, in an unshared silence, before I found something that seemed worth saying.

"You said once, when we first knew each other— can it be less than three months ago?—you said that

I made a good student. Well, perhaps you're right. I do pay attention when it's important to. And I am forty-three years old—that hopefully gives me some perspective about what to pay attention *to*."

"Yes, you've a gift for that, no doubt about it. But there has to be more to it than that. Was anyone in your family . . ."

"Homosexual?" Saying it, I heard that it was the first time the word had been said by either of us to the other. I wondered if it was a word he would not have used, if it was like saying Negro instead of black. But Charles had asked me a question. "I don't think so," I said. "But then, I might not know. I had an uncle who never married. The best raconteur in a family of good story-tellers."

"A sure sign," Charles said, and I thought that smile an honest one.

"There is *something*," I said. "If you need to analyze it. It was something I heard once . . . it struck me. It was in a play by Enid Bagnold. The language was extraordinary. But people want ordinary language in their plays these days. It didn't run long. This woman . . . patrician . . . in her seventies . . . ears and soul as keen as her tongue . . . pays *attention*. Her grandson brings these houseguests down, and this one young man tosses his homosexuality at her, certain she will be . . . not up to handling it. But she just looks him in the eye and says, 'The heart beats.' "

I stopped walking, to make him stop and look at me. I waited until he did, then I said, "That says about all there is to say about human love, doesn't it—'The heart beats'?"

He didn't say a word. He simply looked at me as

though I were a Hindustani phrase. He started walking again, quickly. It was an effort for me to keep up, and then I couldn't any more. I stopped near the first empty bench.

"I can't," I said.

"Would you prefer to go back?" he asked.

"I have to sit down," I said, and I did.

He sat down beside me.

I was tired, decisively tired, so I only know it must have been some time before he spoke. "You know," he said, "that phrase you quoted before, it's an astonishing insight, but what you said, about its being all we need to know about love—Anne, I don't believe that it's that simple. That's why you find me sad."

"I see."

"I don't think so," he said.

If I hesitated, I wouldn't say it. "You feel something for me . . . you can't quite explain to yourself. It doesn't fit in with . . . your history."

"Dear God! Are you a witch? How *could* you know?"

"For a highly intelligent man, you sometimes miss what's right in front—" I shut my mouth tightly on the last word, trying to bite it back. I had said too much.

He stared at me. "It's not possible," he said finally.

"I should think not . . . but it's true," I said. My voice wasn't very steady.

"It's *not* possible."

"Even though it's true?"

"But that boy before . . . God! In these months since . . . there've been a dozen boys like him!"

Why didn't I flinch? He'd said it as harshly as a slap. I was meant to flinch.

Well, I didn't. "Do you think we will bump into every one of them?" I said in a voice whose calmness astounded me every bit as much as it obviously did Charles.

"Still, that's not the point!" he insisted. "That they've existed—that's the point. Don't you see!"

"That in your grief, and pain, and loneliness, you've gone to bed with strangers?" I sighed. I didn't want to remember, but I knew I had to. "Charles," I said, "in the first months after my husband died, I did something worse than go to bed with strangers. I went to bed with . . . friends. Four friends of my husband—four husbands of my friends. Any way you describe it, it's ugly."

"Aren't you evading the point . . . still?"

"Am I? It would hardly have made sense for you to find yourself seeking . . . comfort with women. It wouldn't have been natural."

"No!" He was angry now. "Tell me," he said caustically, "since you seem to understand so very, very much, how can it be that it is with you with whom I feel— most *unnaturally*—at ease, whose company I most *unnaturally* enjoy, whose smile makes me want to smile back." He grabbed my shoulders and began to shake me, his voice rising. "Go on! Explain it all—" A terrible shock slashed his face then. Instantly, his hands let go my shoulders and dropped to his lap. "—away," he whispered. "I'm sorry. I hurt you?"

"A little." I waited. I wasn't sure I was willing to continue this conversation, and was dismayed because it seemed to have a momentum of its own—like a river seeking the sea—to run its course. All right, then. But if we had to go on talking about it, I wasn't going to be edged away from the heart of it by fear of pain.

"Charles, if you want to explain it—explain us—away, I'm sure you can do it. But I won't help you do it—you're on your own."

He searched my face as though it were a map whose accuracy he doubted, but it was the only map he had to go by. "Do you," he said, "have any idea of what we'd be risking? All right, you don't embarrass easily. But you *feel*—God, you've half again more feeling . . . What if I . . . if my history, as you put it, proves stronger than the new, disturbing, disorienting feelings I have for you?

"Anne, I'm forty-four years old and I've never been to bed with a woman. I don't even know if I want to now . . . with you. I don't know if I could. Anne, I want very much to hold you—but maybe that's only to keep you with me, near me. Beyond wanting to hold you—I just don't know.

"And what of your feelings, your needs? You're a beautiful woman—you haven't a shortage of men in your life, men you can be sure . . ." He shook his head. "There are just too many questions."

I was terribly tired. The conversation had already drained me emotionally—and what he said sounded so reasonable . . .

Yet.

"When I was young," I said, "I wanted desperately to have answers, all the answers, to all the questions—immediately. I don't think I've become more patient—patience is not my forte—but I simply know now that it doesn't work that way."

I was feeling my way. I had to make my way through so many feelings, to try to reach him. "Besides," I tried, "having questions, important questions, to which the answers *matter* . . . somehow . . ." Suddenly, I knew what I was trying to get hold of. "Somehow, that proves, I think, that there's still room for beginnings in our lives."

I'd have given five years of whatever life lay ahead for me for one cigarette.

Charles turned toward me, and I didn't turn away, although he didn't speak for so long that I began to want to go home and lie down in a darkened room for ten years or so.

Finally, with the last-second fervor of one who is excruciatingly tempted to change sides in a passionate argument, Charles said, "We'd be taking such a chance! We have too much to lose."

It was true. Much as we wouldn't want it to be, our friendship might be at stake. Feeling that I could not give him the answers to any of his questions—any of our questions—I knew I had only one thing I could give him just then. Time. All the time he needed. All the time in the world if he needed it.

He looked at me, then away, then down, then around. Then his eyes became unfocused, as if he were looking inside himself. When he spoke, at last, he looked at me again, levelly and intently, but there was, after every phrase he spoke, a question mark.

"If we decide to take a chance . . . that has to mean . . . we *have* a chance, doesn't it?"

Despite all the question marks, the one at the end of the question seemed less a question than a stab at hope.

I felt that what I said next, whatever I said, was important. But all I could say was, "I think so."

And *then* the feeling came, and feeling it, I said, "Oh, Charles, I think *so*."

He nodded slowly, as if trying to memorize something. Then he nodded again, differently, as if assenting, as if he had got it now.

As the realization of what we'd agreed to try—the dim, far-reaching, far-fetched open-endedness of it—came upon us, we could only look at each other in wonder at our sheer audacity.

I found the moment unbearably portentous suddenly, and I tried to break it with a smile. But at that instant, a single tear formed and seemed to wedge in the corner of my eye.

He said, "It may take a long time." And then, "It may never happen."

"Yes, I know," I said, making myself know it then.

"You still think it's worth . . . keeping it in mind? I mean, thinking we might have . . . what we have . . . and more?"

"I think so. If you want to."

"I . . . want to. But there's so much we don't know. It seems too much not to know all that. One thing, Anne, there is one thing I must know. Will you tell me?"

"If I know."

"Are you as afraid as I am?" Charles asked.

Nothing but the truth would do. "Yes," I said.

That one dumb tear of mine unlodged itself and started down my cheek.

"Thank you," he said.

He reached out his hand and wiped my tear away. It felt like a caress.

A Beginning:
November, Again

. . . HE NODDED AND STOOD, and without taking his eyes off mine, disposed of his clothes without a wasted motion. He came toward me, and as I moved toward the center of the bed to make room for him, in my excitement and tension I looked the one place I had determined not to look.

But it was all right: he was fully erect. Only then did I know how much of my trembling had been bound up with fear that he would not be ready when the time came. Joyously, I moved into his embrace and felt his body, hard and strong and urgent, pressed against the length of mine. Suddenly, in less time than can be told, the hardness was gone.

And the lifeblood went out of me, too.

For a second his body was still there, against mine, but it had become flaccid. Not just his penis, but the whole of him. At the far edge of that single second, I felt him begin to edge away from me. My disappointment flowed over me in waves, high and threatening. Somehow his disappointment seemed to wash over me, too. The weight of them both was almost too much for me.

I reached out for him. Holding on to him, holding him, it was all the same to me, and it wasn't much. I could taste it: the sharp, salty taste of hope cast overboard.

I let the failure wash over me like grief, and then I made myself get on top of it, ride with it.

A breath. Another.

I tried to recall what we had had before this failed love-making tore the bottom out of everything.

Five months of getting to know one another, a growing friendship, and trust. Shared laughter. A hundred glances interchanged. But now I had nothing to hold on to except the body beside me, and I knew that wasn't enough.

Yet I had to trust my instinct to hang on to Charles. I had to trust me. Forty-three years of living had not gone down some cosmic drain.

All right. I had been with a man who had become suddenly, inexplicably impotent before. Hal. And he, I remembered, was embarrassed when, on occasion, this happened. Childishly embarrassed, as if he'd wet his bed. A grown man was only as strong and big and able . . . as his erect penis.

So Hal had felt . . . not embarrassment, as I had with appalling ease assumed, but shame and anger and rage. No wonder he had, the few times it happened, retreated from my kindly, conscientious unconcern. It hadn't mattered to him that I had not been distressed. The "failure" had mattered to *him*.

How much more, then, must it matter to Charles . . .

I realized that only his indomitable courtesy was keeping him from leaving that bed. Relaxing my hold on him, I made very sure not to move away from him. If he moved away now, it must not be because he felt me retreating. If I were wrong about the sheer weight of irrevocable good manners that was keeping him beside me, well . . . he was a grown man, he would do what he had to do.

I felt relief that it was not in my power to hold him

there. If he stayed, he was choosing to stay. He was free to leave; he was free to stay.

He moved. But only onto his back, his head resting on his arms crossed behind him. He didn't seem to be waiting for anything. Waiting implied expectations. And I suspected that at that moment Charles didn't have any.

He said nothing; neither did I. If there were words to say, I had no idea where to find them—was pretty sure I didn't know the language of that country anyway. If I didn't know what to say, I certainly didn't know what to do. If there was anything to *be* done. I felt intuitively that to do any one of the hundred wrong things I might pick to do would be worse than doing nothing.

Lying still beside Charles, I made myself go back in my head to Charles and me in the other room, to what had happened between us there. Had I read it wrong, had it been my idea and not his to start, to come in here, to touch, to *try*? To *want*? Had he not really wanted me?

It had been many weeks since we had dared to consider the possibility that we might one day become lovers. We had not spoken of it since. We had gone on as before. Perhaps we had been conscious of growing closer. But mostly we had just been together as before. The time hadn't come.

Until tonight.

He had chosen tonight.

Dear God, he had meant to give me himself as a birthday present. Suddenly, I knew that as surely as if he had told me.

Still, he wouldn't have dared, unless . . .

He *had* wanted me: there was no way a man could

falsify that. The heart could lie, the mind could lie, the mouth could lie, but a man's body was, in this sense, an innocent. It didn't know how to lie. He had, if only for a moment, wanted me.

For a moment, yes.

Not long enough.

Time was against Charles. Against us.

If tonight he had wanted me, against that were all the times he hadn't wanted a woman, any woman. All the times, the lifetime, he had wanted—and had—a man.

I could hear Charles's watch ticking beside my ear.

Time.

"You know too little about me," he said then, as if he, too, was hearing the time tick by, and he must do something about the silence it interrupted with such disconcerting regularity. "Only some facts. As an historian, I value facts but do not overrate them. All the facts about a period, neatly entered on index cards laid end to end, do not tell the story, let alone the whole and true story, of that time. The real historian is an artist whose special talent is to re-create what it *felt like* to live then. The gift is rare. I hope—I pray—that I have enough of it at this moment. Because I want to tell you, not more facts about my life, but what it has felt like."

I felt it would be presumptuous of me to protest. I don't think it would have stopped him, in any case.

"You see, one's history is never past—at least, not until it is over. My history is present here, right now, between us. It is what is keeping us apart."

Charles looked up at the ceiling and didn't speak again for some time. I waited.

"I am drawn to you . . . in many ways. But I have been drawn many times by others with whom there was only a single connecting thread, and yet it was able to draw me in with the merest tug. The first time I was drawn like that, I was pulled—reeled in, so to speak —clear across the aisle of a trolley car. When the trolley got to my stop, I couldn't get off. I felt bound to the seat.

"At the last stop the lead was yanked, and I followed it—and the boy who held it—down past the end of the tracks, inside a dark shed where blinding lights went off in my head by which, for painfully splitting seconds, I saw . . . myself.

"That is to be drawn. Drawn and quartered. There was in that boy a darkness, a blackness I found irresistible. He humiliated me and hurt me and gouged my body and my spirit. Yet he made time stand still for me. His penis was a weapon he first used on me, and then made me learn to use. His lips were soft and full, and when he chose, they could kiss with a tenderness which tormented me more than his customary bruising assaults on my body. I could no more have left him voluntarily than I could have willed to stop breathing."

He paused. I thought he might have decided to stop there, but I waited. After a time he went on, his voice roughened now, as if his throat contained an old scar.

"He left me, without warning, without a goodbye, after two years. One Tuesday he enlisted in the merchant marine. I heard it from a boy who didn't even know I knew him. I never saw him again, but he left his mark on me, Sparks did—yes, he had a name. Actually, his name was John Joseph McReady, but no one called him anything but Sparks.

"Try to understand that it was not so much my memories of him, but my memories of what I had been like with him, that stayed with me and nurtured what became my well-developed need for the Sparkses of this world."

Again, silence. I didn't feel the need to hear more, but his need to tell me was almost palpable. There was nothing for me to do but listen, and wait, and listen, and wait. As he talked, the physical tension of failed sex lessened and finally dissipated altogether. After a time, which didn't feel like empty time to me, Charles began, again, to talk.

"I met many Sparkses—from the time on the trolley car, two weeks before my fourteenth birthday, until I met Raymond. I was thirty-eight when I met him, he was twenty-nine. And I had long since given up looking for him.

"We met quite by accident. Not by 'designed' accident the way most of my Sparksian encounters have been precipitated, but truly by chance. An elderly aunt of mine was sick—"

"The one who used to take you to the opera?" I don't know what made me interrupt to ask that; it hardly mattered. But when Charles nodded, he looked . . . touched that I had remembered her.

"A young cousin of Raymond's had the other bed in my Aunt Sybil's hospital room. Both Raymond and I were rather faithful visitors: I loved my aunt and Raymond adored his cousin Marvella. Inevitably we arrived during the same visiting period, and were introduced by my aunt and his cousin, who had made friends, the way people do in hospitals, with spectacular rapidity.

"That first time we exchanged the usual, perfunctory remarks. But when we met after that, we would sometimes take a cigarette break in the visitors' lounge. Once we went down to the coffee shop and had a cup of coffee together.

"It might have just been part of that limbo environment characteristic of cruise ships and hospitals. Except that I had fallen in love with him the first time I saw him. He had been reading Yeats aloud to Marvella when I arrived. After we had been introduced, he went back to reading to her. He didn't read particularly well, but I had the feeling that he would read the book through if Marvella showed the slightest sign that it would give her pleasure. There was this extraordinary gentle quality he had . . . and he was quite beautiful.

"Raymond showed no sign that he was interested in me, or even that he guessed my interest.

"Then my aunt, who was eighty, got inexplicably better, and was discharged. I came to take her home, and while I was settling her back into her apartment, Marvella died.

"She had been showing steady improvement—but it was a tricky blood condition and I guess they really didn't know much about it. Anyway, Raymond had gone for a cigarette. He was just finishing it, in the visitors' lounge, when they came and told him. She was twenty-four years old.

"I didn't know, of course. After I got my aunt comfortable and did a bit of marketing for her, I went home. I was feeling extremely low because although Raymond and I—along with my aunt and Marvella—had exchanged addresses, I had small hope that he would get in touch with me. And it was never my way to take the initiative. Anyway, I found him sitting on my stoop. I lived on Eighty-sixth Street then.

"Without a word he followed me upstairs. He sat

down, without removing his coat, and told me what had happened. I got him to take his coat off, and I poured him two fingers of Scotch.

"He spent the night crying in my arms. There was of course no sex between us that night. It did not occur to him; it occurred to me a dozen times, but I restrained myself totally. He had come to me for comfort—largely because I had been one of the last people to see Marvella alive. If he was going to come to me for me, he would have to decide that. And he was in no state that night to decide anything.

"Still, I felt happier holding him that way, like a mother her son, than I had known I could feel.

"The next morning he went for his things. He knew he didn't have to ask me. He just told me he would be back in an hour, and I knew he meant to stay.

"I did not dare dream he was coming for good, but it *was* for good. I had never shared an apartment with anyone for more than a long weekend. We were together six years. We were temperamentally different, and we looked at the world differently. Raymond was nine years younger than I was, and from time to time he would go away for a day or two . . . adventuring. But he never really left me—I mean he never said he wouldn't be back. And he always did come back. I loved him more, perhaps, than he loved me, but he loved me enough for me. It was a . . . very special relationship."

Charles lay still then, obviously spent emotionally. I felt wrung out myself. I needed a chance to absorb what he had told me—time to find out what I felt about it.

Shocked. The word came to mind instantly, but there wasn't any feeling to give it substance. In my mind's eye I made myself picture the images Charles's story evoked. Of what they *did*. He and Raymond. He and Sparks. He and uncounted others. All I felt was that bodies are bodies and what does it matter how they interlock when they meet?

And I had memories of my own. Memories that I knew I must share. Now.

"A month after Hal died," I said, speaking very low so that Charles would be sure that what I was telling him I had never before told any person, "a month after he died, Alex was away visiting her grandmother for a week. She had been away three days then, when I thought, late one afternoon, that if I stayed home one more hour, if I were alone there for fifteen minutes more, I would start to *howl*. Whether in rage or madness, I didn't know, but I wasn't about to wait and find out. I didn't dare. I combed my hair, put on lipstick, and went out.

"I had no place in mind, not even a direction. I just started to walk. A few blocks from where we lived, I passed a likely bar and grill. I'd been there a few times with Hal. Never in the daytime, of course. I stopped and looked in the window. There were people inside. I went in.

"The bartender said hello. I'd never been in there, or in any other bar, alone before and I was glad he seemed to remember me. When I hesitated, he asked if I'd like to sit at a table, and I nodded.

"He came over to the table, took my order, and brought my drink. I guess he could tell I was uncomfortable—he asked if my husband was away. I said yes, and he went back to talking to a man at the bar.

"The man he was talking to looked vaguely familiar to me. Maybe he lived in the neighborhood. Maybe he just had that kind of face. Anyway, every few minutes he'd glance over at me. When the bartender moved away to wait on another customer, the man got up and came over to my table and asked if he could buy me a drink. I said I had one already. He said did I mind if he joined me anyway. I decided that I didn't mind, one way or the other, and I motioned to him to sit down.

"He was a cheerful man, maybe a little forcefully so for my taste, but he was also a talker, and that suited me. When he told me that he was a salesman, I didn't say that I'd guessed. Instead, I said that I bet that was interesting. He agreed enthusiastically, and then he told me what it was like on the road. Mostly funny stories. Still, it didn't sound like a satisfying life . . . for a family man. That was how he put it. He even showed me pictures—color snapshots of a woman and two boys. He only got home to Utica once a month for a few days. He didn't have any complaints about that, or any of it.

"He said that he liked me, and I believed him. I suppose he liked everybody—that's a salesman's real stock in trade, isn't it? Not my sort of person, but he was a nice man. Larry, his name was.

"He insisted on guessing my name. He guessed Margaret and then Ellen and then Anne. I told him he was a good guesser, my name was Ellen. He was pleased.

"That called for a drink, he said, and I agreed. After some more road stories and another drink for him but not for me, Larry said that the bartender recommended the lasagna. Would I join him? I wasn't hungry, but I let Larry order us the lasagna and garlic bread and some wine. It wasn't bad, and I ate most of mine. He drank most of the wine, but it didn't seem to affect him.

With such an outgoing personality, how can you tell, anyway? I had two glasses of wine myself, and I was feeling decidedly less tense than when I came in.

"When Larry asked if I lived nearby, I instantly tensed up again. Then I thought being alone in the house was driving me crazy . . . and he's a nice man. Why not? I said, I don't live too far away. Larry smiled, paid the check, and left a big tip.

"As we walked out, I glanced over my shoulder at the bartender. He looked surprised. But then I decided it must be my imagination, it couldn't be that easy to shock a bartender.

"We walked slowly. He didn't seem to be in a hurry. At street corners, Larry took hold of my elbow lightly, and when we got to the other side of the street, he let go. I hadn't told him where I lived, only that it wasn't far and— I don't know what made me do it— maybe I didn't want him to be able to find it again . . . I don't know, but I took him a roundabout way. It took at least ten minutes longer that way, and my head was beginning to clear by the time we got to my street. I looked down at my hand—I was holding my keys. I didn't remember taking them out. Larry was talking— another road story—and so I caught him completely by surprise when I suddenly began to run. That head start was what got me to my house and inside the door by the time Larry caught up with me.

"I bolted the door. He rang the bell a few times, and then he called, not yelling but loudly enough so that I could hear him clearly through the door. 'Hey, Ellen, what's up! What's up!' I didn't answer. He began to bang on the door. 'You open up!' he screamed. 'I bought you dinner. You open this door!'

"You'd think one of my neighbors would come help—call the police, do *something*—everyone knew I was alone now. But . . . nothing. Maybe because he was calling 'Ellen' they didn't realize it was happening to me, maybe they all had the TV on. He kept banging on the glass part of the door. I was afraid he might break it. I thought of calling the police myself—but I was afraid of that, too. What would I say when they came? What would *he* say? Then I realized that he had stopped banging, and after a moment I could hear him—not very clearly—complaining that his hand was sore and no woman was worth it. He went away.

"It was then that I began to cry. I didn't know why . . . I mean he was gone. But I couldn't stop."

I was trembling now, and near tears. "Anne," Charles said, "you don't have to put yourself through—"

"That isn't the end of the story," I said.

"It doesn't matter."

"It does to me. I had to talk to someone, to tell someone—someone who would tell me that I wasn't crazy. I went to the phone and dialed my friend Connie's number. She wasn't a really close friend—not close the way Munch is—but she was open, and I thought of her as being sort of sophisticated. Besides, she lived only a couple of blocks away, and I was hoping she'd offer to come over.

"Stew, Connie's husband, answered—Connie wasn't home. She had taken the kids and gone to stay with her mother for a few days. Could he do anything? I sounded really upset, he said, and after all, what were friends for. I said no, really, and he asked was I sure, and I started crying all over again, and he said he'd be right over.

"When Stew got to my house, not more than ten minutes later, I felt really . . . happy . . . to see him. That was funny, because I didn't particularly like Stew. I didn't dislike him. I had just always found him a little . . . aloof. He had a very good job with a big brokerage house in the city; he was always the last man in a crowd to take his jacket off. Now I hadn't seen him since the funeral, although Connie had come over two or three times since then.

"First thing, he apologized for that—for not coming over before. Then he made me sit down and he made me a drink and one for himself, and he sat down beside me on the sofa and made me tell him what had happened.

" 'You poor kid,' he said when I had finished. 'You poor, sweet kid.' He stroked my hair and then he took off his jacket and held my head against his shoulder. I felt comforted. Stew wasn't aloof, I realized, he was just shy. And kind.

"When he kissed me, I let him. I had this detached feeling—about how understanding and sympathetic he was being. How unjudgmental. The least I could do was kiss him. There was no harm in that—a friendly, neighborly kiss—if that was what he felt was right."

I caught my breath, but hurried on. "That wasn't all he wanted, though. By the time I realized what he had in mind, I was spread-eagled on the floor and . . . I didn't make a fuss. Where could I run? I was home. Whom could I call this time? So I just let him. I wasn't really there on the floor anyway. I was standing off to the side, watching Hal's poker crony pounding away at Hal's widow, on Hal's carpet—like a drunk driver pumping away at a horn.

"When he was finished, he looked at his watch and

said he was honest-to-Jesus sorry but he had to run. Connie always called around ten-thirty and it was nearly a quarter past. He was sure I'd understand. Besides, there'd be other times, he assured me.

"The following night my phone rang every half-hour until about nine-thirty. I didn't answer. I didn't do much of anything. I couldn't—I had the lights off in case Stew decided to stop calling and drop by. Steeped in self-pity, I went to bed early and didn't get up until two the next afternoon.

"That night the phone didn't ring even once. Either Connie was back or Stew had lost interest. I didn't care which.

"A few weeks later I was adjusting the temperature of my bedtime bath when the hot-water faucet came off in my hand. I had been having trouble sleeping, and a late-night bath had seemed to help. I tried to remember where the valve was so I could turn off all the water in the house, but I was a blank. I couldn't let the water just run all night—I'd never be able to fall asleep.

"I concentrated, but I still couldn't remember. Maybe I'd never known. Was is possible? I'd lived in that house for six years and I didn't know where to turn the water off? Hal had died without telling me! Damn him!

"It was past midnight. I decided that the only person I could call at that hour was Arnie Marks. He was an obstetrician as well as a gynecologist—mine, as a matter of fact—and he must be used to late-night calls. Naturally, if he was just my gynecologist, I wouldn't have called him. But he was part of Hal's poker group too, and he and his wife Irene sometimes went to the theatre with Hal and me. Nobody else in our crowd liked off-Broadway.

We were friends. And it was an emergency, even if it wasn't a medical one.

"When Arnie answered the phone, I explained the fix I was in, and he laughed and said he'd be right over. He didn't sound put out.

"Arnie arrived within twenty minutes and he knew right away where to turn the water off. He also knew how to put the faucet back on. I told him not to bother, I'd call the plumber in the morning. But he said it wasn't really a big deal, and so I got out Hal's toolbox, and Arnie replaced the faucet.

"He asked if I had any coffee. I pointed out that it would take a while and wouldn't Irene be wondering what was taking him so long. Arnie laughed. His night-time calls generally took longer. Of course. I put a pot of coffee on. Besides, he said, Irene was the ideal doctor's wife. When he got a call during the night, she was asleep again even before he got his clothes on.

"When the coffee perked, I set out some cake, too, and we sat at the kitchen table and talked. It struck me that it was the first time Arnie and I had ever talked alone—except in his office, of course, and that was never for very long because I had never visited him except for my annual checkup.

"I wasn't tired, exactly, but Arnie seemed keyed up and he did most of the talking. He really loved his work, he said. It was so . . . productive. He laughed. I smiled. He told me that most babies weren't born during the night, and that women should all wear cotton panties— it was healthier and healthy was sexy. He also told me that I had among the best . . . boobs . . . of any of his patients.

"I knew, that instant, that Stew had told him. No

wonder he'd been so gallant about paying a plumbing house call in the middle of the night. I got up from the kitchen table and I told him to get the hell out of my house. He just sat there and looked up at me. Until that moment I'd always thought of Arnie as having a kind face, a patient-looking face. Now he didn't appear kind, but he did look patient. He knew there was nothing I could do without coming off like a total fool, or worse.

"After a minute or two, in which he let that idea sink in, he suggested we go upstairs to my bedroom. He wanted to make this very special for me, he said. He understood how lonely I was better than I did myself. We'd wake Alex, I said, if we went upstairs. Ever since her father died, she'd been a fitful sleeper. He looked sympathetic and relented, settling for the living-room sofa."

I really didn't want to tell Charles the rest, but I had to. I had to make him understand what it had been like for me.

"Arnie made me take my clothes off. He told me not to be shy. After all, he'd seen me naked before. I wanted to vomit, remembering how I'd always heard that you shouldn't think of it that way in a doctor's office. I took my clothes off. Arnie took his off and laid them neatly across a chair. He turned to me. His penis was erect and . . . very small. He smiled, told me to lie down, and got on top of me. That son of a bitch sure knew a lot about a woman's insides. He knew what to do in there. I tried hard to think of something else—anything else—but I couldn't. How I hated him for that! He knew how to make it last, too—I came twice. I tried to hide it, but I'm sure he could tell. He . . . preened as he was getting dressed to leave.

"Of course I vowed I'd never set foot in his office again, and I never have. But he . . . made another house call later that week, and twice more soon after. I let him in. Afterward I always felt like dirt. Finally, the last time, I begged him not to come back any more, and he said okay, it was no skin off his nose. And he didn't come back.

"But he stayed in my head. I'd grown to hate him. For the first time in my life, sex with someone was something apart. I couldn't cope with that. I wished Arnie was dead. Mainly because he'd set off this craving in me and I didn't like myself much that hungry.

"I couldn't help myself, though. I sat down and did some figuring. I decided that Arnie wouldn't be likely to talk to anyone about *his* visits to me. After all, most of our friends' wives went to him and they might begin to wonder. Stew *had* talked, and that meant—I was only guessing, but I felt sure—that all the poker players knew. I jotted down their names on separate little pieces of paper, put them in a deep bowl, and picked one out. It was Roger. I called him, and he . . . responded with alacrity. I was right. He didn't even hint that he knew about Stew, but you could tell. He was a nice man, but not much compared to Arnie. A few weeks later I did the names-in-a-bowl thing again, and came up with Curt. He came right over in the middle of the afternoon. He was an insurance salesman and he could make his own hours. He stayed until past nine o'clock and only left when it became clear that I wasn't going to offer him dinner."

Charles didn't say anything, or even move. Neither did I. I lay there, and wondered whether there was more that needed to be said. I felt very tired. There was just a little more, though.

"The morning after Curt's visit, I discovered I had lice. I didn't know that was what it was, but I have ridiculously sensitive skin and by midmorning I was ready to climb the walls. I thought of calling Curt to ask him what it was, but I didn't really know him well enough. Besides, what if he didn't have it? Maybe it was something that took time to incubate and I'd actually caught it from Roger some weeks earlier. The speculation was driving me as crazy as the itching. I called a dermatologist, said it was an emergency, and he saw me that afternoon.

"The doctor asked me a few questions and I told him a few lies. He nodded as though he believed me, and wrote out a prescription for Kwell Shampoo. In two hours I was fine. It was over. So was my sleeping around. But there's no Kwell Shampoo to rid you of the self-disgust that follows sleeping with your husband's friends —with men you thought were *your* friends. What happened between me and those four . . . friends seems to me the very opposite of an act of friendship. And friendship has something to do with sex—it did with Hal and me."

I looked at Charles for the first time since I had begun to speak. "A person doesn't have that many real friends in a lifetime. What I wanted you to know," I said, "is that sex with a . . . friend, the way I had it with those men, seems much worse to me than sleeping with strangers." It had taken me a long time. I had gone a circuitous route. But I had said it, and now I was quiet.

Waiting. For a sign, from him or from inside myself, of where we were. Suddenly, I was very sure that the next move was up to me.

I lay there and let my mind go. What should a woman feel when she found herself in bed for the first time with a man who'd been to bed only with men? It wasn't an everyday situation, obviously, but surely it happened. She should feel . . . whatever she felt. Something was eluding me. She should forget that he was used to . . . no! She should remember . . .

I turned, raised my body slightly and leaned over Charles and kissed his neck—tiny bites of the lips from his ear to his shoulder. I moved a little higher and ran the tip of my tongue along the outline of his lips, then along the place where they met, then . . . quickly away.

To his chest. Which I lightly kissed, and then less lightly, I kissed his nipples. Not lightly at all, I sucked first one and then the other.

I moved from place to place along his body, wherever instinct led me, surprising myself again and again. I did not pause to gauge his reaction to anything I did. I did not ask him, even with my eyes, if he wanted me to go on. If he wanted to stop me, he'd stop me.

I pressed the high part of my palm against the flat of his stomach in a kneading motion. I played with his navel and then I kissed his neck again. I was not playing: red marks came up immediately on his fair skin. I didn't stop.

I touched the hair inside his nostril with my finger and then I flicked the tip of my tongue inside there.

It tasted salty and sweet, and I would have wondered at that but there wasn't time. I had somewhere else to do.

When my mouth found his penis, I ran my tongue up and down the underside—only the point of my tongue and ever so lightly—until I felt that thing begin to stir and lift and fill. I moved my mouth down on it then, and up, and nearly out, and down to the end again, and again out to the tip, and as it filled my mouth, I began to feel the power in me and that if I kept it up . . . But I didn't mean to finish there. I let it go.

And moved, and moved him, and was behind him. I stroked his back with my hands, pressing down, feeling the ribs, the muscles, the astonishingly firm flesh of him. And on down, working the compact roundness of his ass. And on down his hips, and then back, fingertipping his thighs, and up, slowly . . . lightly . . . closer.

Then I ran a finger along in there, between his tight buttocks, up . . . and down . . . and up . . . and down . . . lightly, lightly . . . centering in finally on his anus.

Suddenly, the whole thing changed. Whatever instinct had been telling me where to go, what to do, was gone —replaced by another, new and fierce. I hardly knew what I was doing. I had never done . . . never even thought of doing it before. Now something was happening deep inside me, too. I didn't care any more how it felt to him—I wanted more . . . and more . . . and . . .

Then he moved. He must have guessed what was happening to me—and that made it happen for him. In one motion he pushed me onto my back, and then he was on me, and I felt that thing—big and hard— rubbing . . . pushing . . . pounding against me. And then—suddenly, sharply—it was in me, and he was moving inside me, straight into me, and then drawing out to the very tip of him, and then bull's-eye dead into me, all the way up, and then out a little ways, and around in a circle—lightly, tormentingly lightly—and then out all the way, and then into me—right through me—until I thought he'd break through the skin of my back. I gasped. "Anne?" He knew my name. "Yes! I'm fine! Don't stop!" I cried. The joy of his knowing me seemed to burst inside me. I rose and arched my back to meet him. And I was moving with him and we were together, and together, by God, we were making it. Love.

I did not sleep. I didn't want to sleep, and perhaps dream that it was all a dream.

Besides, I was exhausted beyond sleeping.

I lay beside him, our bodies not touching, not even our hands. I did not feel the need to touch, to confirm that we were there together, that it had happened.

It had happened.

Yet the specifics of our love-making were already fading from my mind. It made me remember how, only an hour after Alex had been born, I had tried to recall exactly how birthing her had felt and could not. I could remember only that it had been excruciatingly hard work, requiring responses I had not known I had in me, and of it I had a daughter.

Now, again, only the result was clear to me. We had made love. It was enough to know, that.

We lay in that untouching silence for a time, I don't know how long a time, and then he slipped out of bed. I turned slightly and watched him go, naked, from the room. He moved unselfconsciously. And I knew then that there would be no need for diminishing reassurances, and I was glad. Dimly, I heard a brief, whirring sound, and then he returned, holding a single glass.

"There was only this much left. We'll share it," he said, sliding into bed beside me. He held the glass to my lips. I drank a little and licked the sticky sweetness of the daiquiri from my lips.

He moved the glass to his mouth, then stopped, and said, "We should drink to something."

"We are," I said.

He smiled then, and drank.

"Did you turn off the oven?" I asked.

"Yes."

"Is the casserole dead?"

"I didn't look," he said, and then, in amazement, "You would have looked."

I nodded. "I'm a domesticated animal," I said.

"Not all that domesticated."

Remembering my passion, I could not meet his eyes, but I answered, "No, not all that domesticated."

He put down the glass. "You were beautiful," he said. "You are beautiful." And he kissed me on my forehead and then he lifted my face and kissed my mouth and then again, and wanting him pushed itself through my tiredness. He moved away ever so slightly and took my face between his hands and said, "We *should* wait until we're a little less tired, shouldn't we? There's time." And then, in a different voice, "There is time?"

"All the time there is," I said.

He lay back against the pillows, fitting my head into the crook of his arm. Neither of us said anything for a time then, until he said, "I feel . . . extraordinary. And yet . . . I don't feel very different."

"I do," I said.

"Will you tell me something?"

"Yes."

"Is there anywhere another woman like you?"

I hesitated only a moment. "No," I said, glad only God could see my face.

About the Author

TOBY STEIN was born in New York City in 1935. She was educated there: at the High School of Performing Arts, where she studied drama; and at Barnard College and Columbia University, where she earned degrees in history. She has been writing most of the time since—mostly for a living. She lives in Montclair, New Jersey, and is at work on her new novel.